This Is the House That Luke Built

This Is the House That House That Luke Built

VIOLET BROWNE

Edited by Bethany Gibson.
Copy edited by Paula Sarson.
Cover and page design by Julie Scriver.
Cover image: *Pieced Together*, copyright © 2022 by Jessica Joy Studio, Instagram @jessicajoystudio.
Printed in Canada by Friesens.
10 9 8 7 6 5 4 3 2 1

Library and Archives Canada Cataloguing in Publication

Title: This is the house that Luke built / Violet Browne.
Names: Browne, Violet, author.
Identifiers: Canadiana (print) 20220405387 | Canadiana (ebook) 20220405395 | ISBN 9781773102832 (softcover) | ISBN 9781773102849 (EPUB)
Classification: LCC PS8603.R6976 T55 2023 | DDC C813/.6—dc23

Goose Lane Editions acknowledges the generous support of the Government of Canada, the Canada Council for the Arts, and the Government of New Brunswick.

Goose Lane Editions is located on the unceded territory of the Wəlastəkwiyik whose ancestors along with the Mi'kmaq and Peskotomuhkati Nations signed Peace and Friendship Treaties with the British Crown in the 1700s.

Goose Lane Editions
500 Beaverbrook Court, Suite 330
Fredericton, New Brunswick
CANADA E3B 5X4
gooselane.com

To my mom,
Geraldine Violet Browne,
for mothering me

And to my children,
Meg, Will, and Emily,
for surviving my mothering
and loving me anyway

And even in our sleep, pain which cannot forget falls drop by drop upon the heart until, in our own despair, against our will, comes wisdom through the awful grace of god. —Aeschylus

Contents

October

The first time Rose walks through the wall is on the second anniversary of Luke's disappearance.

Rose steps through the living-room wall of the house that Luke had started to build for them, to find him stretched the length of the couch, his elbow propped on the arm. He is covered in a purple patchwork quilt. Luke pulls his knees up and throws the blanket aside for Rose. She strips to her undies, pink and baby-blue flowers against a dark background, the bra trimmed with lace. She has had a pedicure, nail polish in the same powder blue. Rose wiggles her foot in Luke's direction.

See my toes.

You have nice toes, Rosie. Lovely toes.

Rose plumps the bed pillow Luke put on the opposite end of the couch for her, settling in, and he reaches to give her big toe a tweak. She aligns the pads of her bare feet flat against Luke's and they push sole against sole, each bending to the pressure of the other's forward thrust, like pedalling a bike.

Myself and Cela could do this for hours when we were kids.

Sure, you're still only a youngster, hun.

Rose sits upright to sip her glass of Merlot, dark and bitter as coffee. She cracks a piece of Luke's orange chocolate Aero bar and pops it into her mouth.

See, you still have your sweet tooth even. Barely out of your teens.

Luke shifts position, his feet pointing toward his own pillow, his head nestling into Rose's lap. She feels the weight bearing down, the warmth of his hand burrowing into the space between his cheek and her thigh. As he settles, Rose sweeps her fingertip slowly along the path of Luke's lashes, traces the curve of his brow. Her fingers absorb every line on his face, hesitate at the pulse in his temple.

Luke slides his hand upward, pushing the flowered polyester out of his way. He tattoos her hip with his lips, whispers hieroglyphics onto her skin. Luke pulls Rose to lie beneath him, her body arching to meld with his. Becoming a part of his muscles and his sinew and his bones.

Molecules

Ever since her father vanished when she was fifty-three days old, Emily's body has been gripped by a vibration at the molecular level. It hums. Certain combinations of matter spark sentience within the molecular structure as a whole; take water, add some carbon and nitrogen and a couple handfuls of trace elements and these molecules may, as in Emily's case, spend a human life in search of paternal connection. Her body defies the established bounds of physics, biology, logic, in favour of a genetically driven, atomic keening—Emily is compelled to map its surface in piercings and tattoos.

There have been lip and nose rings, surface piercings, microdermals. Rose didn't notice until the day Emily came home flaunting the shiny ball above her lip, her friends trailing behind.

You've punched a hole in your face.

Now, Mom.

Emily, you have a hole punched through your top lip. What do you expect me to say? Oh, I can't wait for you to get more? Oh god, Emmy, do you have more?

No, Mom.

I will strip search you in front of everyone if you don't tell me the truth.

Knowing her mother, Emily shows her a double tongue piercing, a belly-button ring, and a tattoo on her left hip that she got in someone's basement.

Rose googles it all. Every time there's an addition to the swelling collection of piercings and surgical steel and script and emblems, Rose goes to her laptop. *Jesus Christ* escapes through her clenched teeth as photos stream past, a forceps with handles like scissors that clamp a tongue in place, impaling it manually with a needle, leaving the tongue swollen, double its normal size. The procedure impairs Emily's speech for days.

The dermal punch is not as scary. A surgical instrument used in biopsies, it is a sharp metal circle, a Barbie–sized cookie cutter. The punch removes tissue to allow an anchor to be implanted in the dermis of the skin, inserted like an upside down *T*, with a glass jewel screwed into a threaded hole at the top. Large holes in the *T*'s base encourage tissue to grow through and around the openings, making it harder to get rid of. The body always fights to repair itself, though, the metal intrusions into flesh. It rushes to fill the space left by a tongue ring dislodged while Emily sleeps, healing it before morning.

Rose watches videos of tattoo guns, small drills driving ink into skin with needles, in and out, in and out, eighty to a hundred and fifty times a second, forcing pigment into the dermis. The immune system's cells coat the intrusive particles, like an oyster creating a pearl. Deep in the skin, granulation tissue forms, the dye trapped at the dermis-epidermis border.

Emily may be practising self-expression. Or she could be self-mutilating. Either way, she's exerting control over her body. And didn't Rose know that already? She learned that even sociologists and psychologists won't label the phenomenon. She learned that it's as painful as it looks. And didn't she already know that too? She'd run her hand down the curve of Emily's back more than once, when she crawled into bed with Rose late at night, and laid her bottle of Aspirin on the nightstand. Rose wishes she knew what to do, to ease the loneliness that wafts off Emily's skin.

Before she discovered the first piercings, she found a tiny plastic bag of white crystals left on the bathroom countertop. She knocked on Emily's bedroom door, her heart beating like a trapped bird trying to flee. Emily promised her mother it was nothing, then accused her of overreacting to every little thing, then finally opened the bag to calm her. The white crystal was a sea-salt blend, used for cleansing and purification; Emily uses it to prevent infection in her piercings. Rose learned that part of the attraction to body modification is the pain itself. Some people need the pain. It releases pressure, provides a path to the surface for the forces welling deep below.

Rose goes with Emily sometimes, now that she knows. Holds her hand. Watches Emily lie prone. Face down. Watches the man's surgical precision as he preps the surface. Watches the needle pierce Emily's skin, pierce Emily's skin, like a sewing machine piecing her together. Hears the long, whistling intake of breath as blues and greens plume across the back of Emily's neck. Feels Emily's fingernails hook in the flesh of her palm. Smooths her hair when it's over. Exhales.

And sometimes Emily has to go alone. When Rose pops home between meetings or dinner dates, she'll find that Emily has wandered down Monkstown Road to Prescott Street again, to see the man. And come home with a boat or a knotted rope forming a scab on her skin. Exhausted. Assuaged for a while. Sometimes she sleeps for two days. Then Rose goes to her laptop. Googles Emily from head to toe.

The microdermal is Rose's favourite now—two silver studs embedded in Emily's clavicle, just above the words *So it goes...* The hip tattoo that was done in a basement is covered now with a boat's steering wheel, set in waves. *Homeward Bound.*

Like on her father's arm. When Rose saw Emily's tattoo she wondered why she chose a different font than her father. It took her seconds to realize that Emily had never seen Luke's tattoo. Emily gets other emblems for him—an anchor on the vein of her wrist, a sailor's knot above her thumb, a miniature boat in full sail on her left arm.

A peacock feather extends from the nape of Emily's neck halfway down her trapezius muscle. Peacocks can ingest poison and not die. There's the quote on her right ribcage about feelings lingering even after memories fade. Ghosts. An owl in shades of grey on her right quad. Omen of death, medium to the dead, intuition. A sugar skull on her ankle—fuchsia and yellow hippie flowers surrounding empty black eye sockets. Google says sugar skulls are used in memorial ceremonies remembering the dead.

Following the curve of Emily's foot, the Cheshire Cat's teeth form a grin above the words *We're All Mad Here*. And on her left thigh there is an unfinished tattoo. Alice is framed in a mirror and falling through the rabbit hole. Aside from her heart-shaped red lips, she is waiting for colour.

Emily's topography is moulded by the dictates of her inner core, welling up, welling up. Her muscles and sinew and bones. It is not only the heart that wants what it wants.

Mermaids

1994

While there are no reports of mermaid sightings at 47° N, 51° W that night, this is easily explained by the fact that the other vessels were tied up or in the lee of the land, when Pat Coates and his crew go down.

The top of the wheelhouse is forced up and over, from port to starboard. The sea surface is five degrees Celsius and the ambient air temperature is eleven. The chance of survival in five-degree sea water is high and a man can help himself for up to thirty minutes. For up to an hour and a half, he has a 50 per cent chance of surviving if rescued. These averages vary, depending on age, physical condition, injuries, and weather. The crew members are all considered experienced fishermen; one is an accomplished swimmer, another can't swim, and the other three can make a few strokes. During the next few hours, boats risk themselves in the severe weather to recover debris, including the wheelhouse top with a section of the front, pieces from the port after side, boxes, dory parts, rope and twine, net-marking balloons, the upright inflated life raft, a brown suede sneaker boot. A section of the vessel's keel, with pieces of ribs attached, drifts away.

Mermaids watch as they always do when these things occur, but they take no ownership in the disaster at sea. They scorn the reputation they've heard, men blaming their own banshee wails aboard sinking boats on beautiful women with fishes' tails.

As the waves surrender their prize to deep ocean, the men descend slowly in water that is colder, denser, darker. It is quieter. The calamitous surface is forgotten as Luke's body drifts in slow motion with the plankton. A tuna darts by, attracted by the sound of the sinking craft. Downward through seaweed and jellyfish, schools of dogfish, dolphins and mermaids hover as he falls away, themselves wary of the sharks, who will no doubt happen by before the debris settles.

There is no personal animosity toward the bodies because of their intrusion here. No thought given to families or unfinished houses. These men will be forgotten. Other men will take their place. They will grow from boys whose mothers will always mourn the moment they belong to another woman, into men who leave their wives and children on wharves as they cast off. Men who marvel at the pull of the water that takes them away from everything they own, bringing them to back-breaking labour and heart-wrenching freedom; who love, are loved, who bicker and argue; who hunt and are hunted; who live and die. It's just the way life is.

The scraps of fishermen churn in Davy Jones's locker. Everything here circulates in a more or less clockwise motion, in an expanding circle, like the ripples from a boy's stone skipping across the water's surface, moving outward and downward simultaneously, settling eventually, if luck holds, and becoming a particle of the continental shelf.

How to Build a Boat

Rose grew up scrambling on wharves and boats, never really absorbing her father's warnings to be careful around the water. The family was resettled from Paradise to O'Rielly Street when she was two, and she toddled the floor of their new house for months, crying to go home. Now her father goes back every spring to fish and they join him when the school year ends. Rose lives for it. Spends summers in the sun that raises the freckles in clusters across her nose. Salt water stinging her nostrils and curling the ends of her hair.

This morning, something of substance must be going up in slips of smoke; no one burns trash in Great Paradise. The smoke rises over the stagehead, reverberating around the harbour. A burning boat. Every man's heart skips a beat. Every wife's hand freezes mid-air. Every child's ear jumps to the raised octave of adult voices. *Jesus Christ Almighty.*

Someone shouts a name. John's boat. Rose's thirteen-year-old legs get her there before anyone else, sprinting over the tattered bridge that crosses the brook, a part of the rocky path around the harbour, past summer cabins that used to be family homes painted yellow and green, a wooden walkway on pilings stretching across dirty shallow water and between flakes,

Rose's eyes never leaving the smoke rising in the background; Cela is close behind. Their feet barely touching down as they fly over the flakes to the wharf.

Fire licks the wheelhouse door, smothering the view of the interior through the window. But it's not as bad as Rose expected. Aside from the wheelhouse—which she's not fond of anyway because of the stink—the boat looks the same as it does on any other day. Rose grabs a bucket and jumps down aboard her, bailing water over the gunwale and tossing it in the direction of the wheelhouse. Half the people in the harbour show up and immediately start throwing opinions into the mix. They take to shouting that Rose has to get up out of her before she blows, and Rose, in the noise and confusion, does as she's told. There is swift decision-making. This is a boat tied up alongside other boats. Never mind the winter's work that went into putting her on the face of this Earth. She's a threat.

Within minutes, the boat is cut loose, a funeral pyre drifting out to the middle of the narrow harbour. Rose doesn't know where her father is standing. And she doesn't know who untied her. There is serenity in the boat's movement as she slips backward away from the wharf, the flames eating her. The crowd eventually disperses, secure in the knowledge of the other boats' safety, and Rose glimpses her father retreating to their house to watch. It takes hours before the boat tips her bow skyward and goes down. Mushrooms of black black smoke rise until the men from The Bight show up to see if everyone is burned alive. And Rose's father stands in the kitchen window, his hand leaning on the sill. Three times, his hand darts to his mouth to try to smother a sound that betrays him, unable to pull himself away.

In the coming days, the boat is stripped of her resting place, dragged along the harbour floor and hauled up in the cove, where gulls comb her empty shell for leftovers and wind and salt air pick her clean. The boat could have been saved; Rose is sure of it. She should've been saved.

Rose had never seen work of her father's hands before the boat. Or if she had, she didn't recognize it and certainly never felt the weight of it. She recalls vague references to his carpentry, watching him slip his cigarette pack back into his shirt pocket at the kitchen table on his lunch break. He was the foreman on a job, building a house for the barber, when he decided to quit smoking—forty-five years and decided that day on his lunch break to stop. Never smoked another cigarette in his life, though he carried the package in his pocket until the tobacco dried and fell out of the tubes. Rose doesn't know if he was really the foreman. She only knows he used to laugh and call himself that, then he'd say there were only two of them working the job. Rose remembers a winter when her mother was excited because he got a real job in Nova Scotia, and he flew over to go to work as a carpenter. Turned out the company doing the hiring hadn't bothered to tell the Newfoundlanders they'd be scab labour, and he flew home with not a cent earned, minus his tools that were stored in a work shed the strikers burned to the ground.

The boat was something Rose knew from its conception. Her father cut the wood for the stem, quarter knees, deadwood, transom, and the timbers. He bought the planks from Lannon's sawmill. There was talk for a long time about the day he found the perfectly curved log for her bow. Rose had no idea where he actually cut the trees, but every time she heard the story of the bowed log, she pictured him combing the hills across the gut, like a hunter. She was mesmerized to think that without his stroke of luck that day, the boat would not have been.

Rose passed the winter she was twelve in Mr. Corcoran's big garden, visiting the boat, dark stripes of oakum and pitch wedged between seams in blond wood. Her father stood on a homemade scaffold at her stern, moulding her proportions to fit the picture of her in his head, wood shavings tumbling around the garden, littering the snow. He had the piles all winter from shinnying her keel. Rose and Cela took turns cutting through gardens and yelling over Mr. Corcoran's fence to tell their father when dinner was ready.

In the spring, a section of fence had to be removed to get the boat out and a few council workers trailed them to the water. Her father was afraid of bad luck launching a boat on a Friday, so he waited until the town council office reopened Monday morning. Then the boat was herded along Wakeham's narrow lane and through the streets of Placentia to the slip past the breakwater. Someone brought a camera to get pictures of her maiden voyage. There is one photo of Rose standing next to Abbey, with Jon in her arms, up forward as they made their way down through the gut. Cela was late and got left behind in the rush; she still tears up sometimes about missing the first ride.

Rose was old enough to be embarrassed by her father's procrastination in cleaning up the neighbour's garden. Mr. Corcoran got tired of asking and did the job himself. Her father was scraping a living, and not having owned much of value in his own life, he didn't quite understand caring for "stuff." The only car he'd ever owned, given to him by his brother, was demolished when Abbey's husband rear-ended her while she was driving it. Rumour was that he'd been tailgating Abbey. Rose's father absorbed the loss so that their insurance didn't go to hell.

But then the boat. He built her thirty-nine feet, six inches long, to avoid the stricter Coast Guard rules and regulations for a forty-footer. She was eleven feet wide and about seven feet from the bottom of her keel to her gunwales, with about a three-foot draft. She was painted a bright white with a dory-green trim and was skirted up to her waterline in red ochre. She looked tall and skinny because her house, instead of extending straight across her width like other boats, stopped short a foot or so on each side, allowing passage from forward to stern.

For six weeks that summer, she was the fastest skiff in Great Paradise harbour. She could do eight knots easy, a sprinter compared to the others. When he took them for rides around the island on his boat, Rose's father would open her up and watch the water shiver in her wake. He wasn't supposed to push her until the engine was seasoned, but a few times he couldn't resist, and he'd grin like a little boy as she responded to his commands. He'd shout over the engine, pointing at the froth she was leaving behind, and Rose would laugh along with him out of the sheer glory of seeing him so excited. On workdays, he came home as happy, the top catch more often than was good for a man's reputation in a small harbour.

Then on a quiet afternoon, fishing done for the day, smoke slipped up over the stagehead and ascended higher over the rooftops of the stages themselves.

Gathering

Rose herself fished once. Her mother was sent in from Great Paradise to the hospital in Placentia with gallstones. So another pair of hands was needed, and Rose spent the day on the water with her father and his shareman. Up at four o'clock, out into cold darkness and the eternal caw of seagulls.

They walk the narrow path single file, grass trodden to a muddy rut along its centre, past Gary's shack with its careless clothesline, to the squeaky wooden walkway that leads to her father's fish stage, its walls of raw board worried by weather. Down over slippery rungs into the skiff, which is always kept freshly painted. Boats are respected here. Bright white, grey trim. Not the ugly shade of battleships, creamy grey like a cashmere sweater.

The Rose was a replacement for the boat that her father had built himself and trimmed in dory green that burned the year she was built. Her father couldn't go through that hurt again, so he commissioned the Grandys in Fortune to build *The Rose*. He said that's what he should have called the boat that he built, the work of his own hands, and he chastised himself over it. As if that could have saved her.

The Rose's length meant she had to be registered with the provincial government, and it was plastered across her arse in the same colour as her name, branding her as an outsider in the bay. *Registration: St. John's.* Rose wondered if the city's name emblazoned on his boat stirred memories of Prescott Street for him, where he boarded as a young man working in town, a world away, before he was theirs.

The engine coughs awake, then roars over the seagulls. Rose settles onto the tawt back aft, goosebumps surfacing as her bum contacts the damp wood. Gary releases the ties, and they head out of the harbour past the breakwater, into quiet. Of a sort. The drone of the engine is a part of the quiet. Black water lapping the bow, lulling Rose to sleep in the dark, cold, quiet of a sort. Boat on water. Like a Christopher Pratt painting.

Two hours' steam brings them to the banks. They fish New Bank and White Sail. Rose expects the banks to be different somehow, to stand out, but they look the same as the whole trip there. Pre-dawn, water is black, baked green as the sun rises higher. Pretty Mediterranean green, sprawling as far as Rose can see. Not another soul. It looks big. And empty.

They cut the engine and a new quiet rises—big and empty. The boat follows the groundswell, barely noticeable on the water's surface, but swaying Rose till she stumbles sideways. She adjusts her stance to the movement, looks around, feels tiny. Like a speck.

Nothing to do but start the process, amid the business like small talk that accompanies the hunt. Gary up front on the deck. Her father in the middle, casting the cod jigger through the wheelhouse door. He leans on its frame, bibbed navy-blue hat and brown woollen plaid coat bobbing to the rhythm of the handline. Rose back aft where she'd ridden. Empty locker staring her in the face, asking to be fed. Rose doesn't want to. She's never given a codfish a second thought in her life. But now she doesn't want to see one.

The closest Rose has ever come to concern for fish was when she was a child and her father took them for a ride around the island in his old punt. She dropped a string with an empty hook over the back of the boat, trying to catch a conner, and snagged one just as they pulled away from the wharf. His mottled turquoise belly, like a glazed flower vase, flopped along on the white wake spreading behind them. Rose wanted to pull the conner aboard to save him the torture he was in, but she was afraid that he would die out of the water. So she left him to suffer in the spray. Once around the island. Twice. Rose had never wanted a boat ride to end. But she longed for it then, longed and hurt with the fish.

Rose tosses the jigger over the side, watches the lead weight rush down into green water, the barbed points of its twin hooks glistening, luring its prey to death. She pulls the handline up and down slowly, as the others are doing vigorously; she is hoping not to catch anything at the same time that she grows impatient with the vast emptiness. They restart the engine, move a few hundred feet along the bank, cut the engine again. Choruses of jagged sound are interlaid with smooth verses of calm.

A bite. Rose pulls hand over hand on the line until the fish comes into sight, hauls him over the side, his silver-and-ivory-mottled skin bristling at the indignity of being chattel. She pulls the hook from his lower lip as she's been shown, the little flap of skin under his chin like a goatee quivering in response. Rose lays the fish in the empty locker and tries to ignore him until he lies still. Just as she thinks he has drawn his last breath of air, he gives another flick, trying to propel himself out of this dry hell. Rose and the fish stare with wide eyes toward the wheelhouse but are granted no relief. The fish will not be released. Rose's father laughs at her, nicely, when she begs clemency for the fish. Another bite. The process repeats and so it goes for a portion of the morning.

The first half-dozen fish object and cajole, gasping for water in the empty locker. As suddenly as Rose became attuned to their feelings, she becomes deaf to their rhetoric. Desensitized. Or sensitized. Rose coaxes the jigger down to tug into flesh. Swims it back to the surface. Hand over hand. Preens as she pulls a large, writhing cod over the gunwale. The process repeats.

When Rose's locker is half full they break for lunch. Fish gurry on her hands joins the flavours of potted meat, home-made bread, butter. One of the best meals she's ever eaten. Her father laughing.

Hunger is good sauce.

After lunch, on they come. Hundreds of pounds of grey-and-beige-speckled meat, combined with her father's and Gary's, becoming thousands of pounds.

Nothing left but the return journey and the gutting of their catch on the way home. Hadn't occurred to Rose that they'd gut on the way in. She's squeamish again. Rose hoists herself down into the centre locker, opposite Gary, knee-deep in codfish jumbled around her mother's rubber boots.

Gary pulls a knife from where it's tucked behind a rib of the boat, its blade curved the shape of a new moon, thinner at the centre and slightly fatter where it nestles into its light wooden handle, fitting his palm perfectly. In what looks like a single motion, he grabs a fish from the locker, slits its throat, runs the blade down through its belly, and slides the fish across the wooden cover of the locker as if he is passing Rose a salt shaker. Laughs at her turning her head away as she sticks cotton-gloved fingers into the wound he's opened. He shows her how to wrap the entrails around two fingers and pluck, just where the slices of the blade intersect under the gills. Rose feels them squishing like raw egg through thin cotton between her fingers. She struggles to right herself against the heavy rocking of the boat. Gulls appear to gather offal as she guts and tosses, guts and tosses. Gary and Rose take turns cutting the throats, pulling the guts, throwing it to the birds.

Two hours of this and they're heading into the harbour. The three lockers yield roughly eight hundred pounds apiece, gut out. Twenty-four hundred pounds of fish. Gutted. Rose's locker holding the single biggest fish of the day.

Leaving

1981

Rose clicks Jon's seatbelt in place and kisses him on the nose.

Off you go. What an adventure.

Abbey is moving to Alberta with her husband for work, taking Rose's nephew away. Jon is six, born on Rose's tenth birthday. Rose is afraid that Jon won't remember her, afraid she'll forget the smell of him. She closes the door, slamming Jon away in the back seat among bags and boxes crammed into every crevice. There is a rack attached to the roof that is piled high, two one-gallon buckets of Old Port salt beef tied in place with heavy cotton rope.

Hold on Abbey, I have to go get something.

Rose goes to her bedroom, takes out the small patchwork quilt she's been working on for home ec, and brings it outside, its reds and yellows bright in the sun. Rose opens the car door again and leans in.

I was making this for you, baby boy.

As she squeezes the unfinished quilt into the seat beside Jon, Abbey's husband says, We don't have room for anything else, Rose. We have plenty of blankets.

Jon fingers the firetrucks and spaceships crowded together on the patches and smiles at Rose.

See. It's tucked in already. Not taking up any room. I made it for him.

Rose offers one last peck on Jon's head and gives Abbey a quick hug before she sprints up the steps into the house, while the others say their goodbyes and wave as the car pulls away and down O'Rielly Street.

Rose can't watch him go.

Meringue

Cela's babysitting while Rose goes on her first real date with Luke. Rose lays the lemon meringue pie on the table, as Cela stands close to the window to catch a glimpse of him when he gets here. It's important to Rose that Cela likes him. They've been best friends their whole lives, even though Cela is younger. When Cela started grade nine, she and Rose sat together in the cafeteria during lunch breaks, and Rose's high school friends were flabbergasted when they found out they were sisters. "You sit with your sister at lunch? Wow. I don't even talk to my sister!"

Rose warned him he would be sized up, but Luke is not the type to come knock on the door and introduce himself, so Cela will have to take her estimate from a distance. And anyway, Rose wants to be sure before he meets Maggie and Liam, who are eyeing the pie themselves.

Mommy has pies in the fridge, guys. Aunt Cela will get you some when I leave.

Rose was delighted when she asked Luke what foods he liked and he said baked ham and lemon pie. She had been getting ready for him her whole life. Her favourite meal to make is baked ham with raisin sauce, buttery mashed potatoes, and pineapple carrots, the smell of the cloves mingling with brown

29

sugar. Rose buys her pie crusts because she knows to concentrate effort where it's needed, and the deep-dish shells in the yellow box are fine. She fills the shell to the top edge with tart lemon filling, then heaps a thick layer of meringue with perfectly peaked whitecaps, droplets of caramelized sugar forming on the browned topping as it cools.

Luke's pickup rolls to a stop, hugging the sidewalk close. Cela stands just left of the window, to stare without being seen. Luke is clean-shaven with a mop of curly dark hair, and he is smiling toward the house.

Looks good, Rose. Looks good.

Rose wipes her right index finger across her front teeth.

Any lipstick? She bares her teeth at Cela.

Nope, you're good.

Quick hugs to Maggie, Liam, and Cela before she balances the pie on one hand and heads out the door. She catches Luke's gaze as she walks around the front of the truck. He leans across the seat and pushes open the door.

What's this? A pie?

Yep. I remembered you said lemon was your favourite.

I think you might be my favourite, too, by the look of this.

Rose sets the pie down and pushes it gently across the seat so that it sits close to Luke, then hoists herself up into the truck and pulls the heavy door closed.

No need to sit so far away, Rose. Luke revs the engine to life. Rose feels like a teenager. Luke stretches his arm across the seatback as Rose gives a little hop closer, then another. On the second hop, Rose's bum lands squarely on the lemon meringue pie, flattening the aluminum foil pan and squishing its contents into the crevices of her jeans and the seat.

Oh my god! Rose lurches for the door handle, her feet on the ground again as her cheeks flush.

Give me a few seconds. Sorry, I'll just be a minute.

Luke lets her go without a word, hiding his laughter behind a raised hand as he watches her hurry up the steps and through the door, before he pulls a few Mary Brown's napkins from his glove locker to clean the seat.

Oh my god! I sat in the goddamn pie. I sat. In the pie. Rose's eyes start to water.

I climbed in the truck and sat in the pie.

Cela stares until a piece of meringue, weighed down with lemon, plops onto the floor from Rose's jeans.

Some sweet, Rosie.

Jesus, Cela.

Just trying to make you laugh.

Well, help me with these will ya. Rose peels the jeans to her ankles and steps out of them.

Go on, I'll get the mess. Grab my new jeans out of the bag there.

Rose gives herself a quick wipe-down in the bathroom and slips into the dark-wash boot-cuts, grateful that they button. Rose is always trying to lose ten pounds.

I gotta call Abbey and tell her this one, Rosie.

Rose heads back to the kitchen, quick hugs all around again before she makes another go of it. She opens the front door, a metal roaster balanced under her arm. Rose catches Luke's gaze as she retraces her steps and pulls the truck door open. She lays the roaster on the seat and pushes it gently toward Luke before she climbs in and makes a little hop on her bum to get closer. Luke reaches to raise the cover and peeks inside. He grins at the lemon meringue pie nestled among dish towels in the bottom of the pan.

You needn't've run off so fast with the last one, Rose. I would've kissed your arse for it.

Rose feels her cheeks go hot.

Oh, you and my sisters will get along. Just fine.

Dandelion

Rose and Luke are getting married in a week, and Rose is having a quiet meltdown in the wrought-iron bed in Cela's blue bedroom. What if she still loves Bill? She can't go marching into another marriage headlong like there's no tomorrow. There is a tomorrow, and a tomorrow after that. There's forever. And Rose is twenty-six and she has a four-year-old and a five-year-old who are depending on her to make the right decisions. What if she's making a mistake? Rose knows what marriage is and she knows what forever means. She needs to be sure. Love doesn't dissipate like fog. Love is more like a dandelion.

A dandelion is a weed, its dominant root thick and tapering; it grows deep quickly, its taproot system spreading away like veins. The dandelion is a common colonizer of disturbed habitats, producing thousands of seeds that spin through the air like tiny parasols. Dandelions are healers. They have fed and healed people since prehistory, a whole world of pharmacology hiding in their leaves like magic. They are hard to uproot, and if broken off near the top, the part that stays in the ground often resprouts. Love is like that.

Rose thinks about the first time she laid eyes on Maggie and Liam's father. Bill was the prettiest thing she ever saw.

Navy Levi's, which had laid folded neatly in a bottom drawer for months before being worn, because you don't wear new jeans to go out; collared periwinkle polo shirt with three buttons, the top one left undone; grey suede-and-fabric jacket with a fastener on its stand-up collar, left unzipped; thick brown hair cut very short, with a side part forcing the strong waves across his head; dimpled chin below full lips that smile without revealing teeth. He was sitting on the railing that ran around the dance floor, thumbs tucked into belt loops, one high-top sneaker balanced on the lower rail, the other planted firmly on the dirty carpet. She saw him watching her, but they'd never have spoken if she hadn't gone and said hello. Rose never really knew what shy was.

And later, Luke.

Rose is out dancing, she and Bill have fallen out for the thousandth time, and she's sick and tired of wanting him to stop leaving every time she throws a plate. His quiet refusal to talk about things, to get things out into the open, makes Rose throw plates. And the plates make Bill retreat. So she lets him slam the door behind him, which drives Maggie and Liam into the little bedroom down the hall in their rental. They're not used to emotion spilling out of their father. And Rose can't bear it pent up.

Luke circles the bar a few times, criss-crossing his way back, slowing as he approaches, and moving on again, until he stops while Rose is ordering a drink, her back facing the crowd. He stands beside her, leans in.

Don't suppose a pretty woman like you would dance with the likes of me, would ya?

She turns and sizes him up, as if she hasn't noticed him until now. Faded jeans and a white T-shirt left untucked. His dark hair is curly, his hairline receding before its time. He smells like soap. He is a burly man, and when he smiles at her the right corner of his mouth arches higher than the left. A strong friendly face. Handsomest man Rose has ever seen.

As Rose plumps Cela's pillow then sinks back into it, she thinks about the night she and Luke went dancing again, a few months after they started dating. Luke had too much to drink so he got a cab back to Rose's house early. Bill was out at the Legion that night too. He had watched Rose and Luke together. Bill offered Rose a ride home when the taxis stopped running. He walked her to the front door where they could see Luke through the window, sound asleep on the couch. Bill lingered on the doorstep. Rose told him to go on, she was fine. She encouraged him to call the girl from down the shore who was interested in him. When he protested, Rose asked him what was wrong with the girl. Bill said, "She's not you." Rose told him it was much too late now, though she'd wanted to hear words like that for a long time. But now it was too late. Her throat ached. And that was as much as Rose would ever hear from Bill about any of it.

Rose thinks about how hard it always was to squeeze Bill's love out, even though she knew it was there. And how easy it's always been with Luke, from the night she and Luke met over a year ago. Easy even before he gave up drinking, when Rose said, I'm too old for this, and I have children who I will not raise like this. So you can have your drink or you can have me, but you can't have us both. And he laid down the bottle.

Luke is carved on the palm of her hand, etched into her muscles and her sinew and her bones. Rose's body hums when Luke is near, and her chest hurts when he is far away. She thinks about Bill and she thinks about Luke, and she knows she loves them both. But she knows Luke is her forever.

Hitchhike

Rose finishes a crazy night at the salon and heads home late, at nine thirty. No Luke. He's somewhere on the highway with Barry. Tried to reach Rose but the phone at the salon was busy for an hour. So he called her mother to let Rose know he and Barry were leaving Bay Bulls by foot. Well. A ride to the turnoff with the skipper and dropped off on the highway. Barry's woman wouldn't drive out for them on a night like this. So Luke and Barry decided to hitchhike, to get a night home, instead of staying aboard the boat. Hitchhike. Grown men. In fishermen's clothes. Rose waits until ten then calls her father.

Can you come with me? I have to go look for Luke. Mom will have to stay with the kids.

Rose and her father get aboard Luke's Camaro, Rose still in her work cape, stinking of the perm solution she's been squirting all day onto hair wrapped in endpapers. Two translucent papers sandwiching the tips of women's hair, rolled onto coloured plastic rods and held in place at the scalp by a black rubber band. The smell gives Rose a headache, to top off the aching feet. They stop for gas before heading out to look for two grown men hitchhiking from Witless Bay Line in the dark.

An hour after they climbed out of Pat's pickup truck and started strolling with their thumbs out at the approach of

35

every vehicle, Luke and Barry are sorry for their bargain. The air is as dense and as wet as rainfall, and cold. The sky fades from indigo to inky blackness the colour of squid juice, the kind of unbroken darkness that causes men to stumble. They curse every car that lights their path only to plunge them back into darkness, as the driver passes without even lifting their foot from the pedal. Luke accepts Barry's offer to share his coat, and shrugs into the heavy green canvas, the heat from Barry's body lingering in its folds. Luke pulls the two sides of the coat together in front, overlapping the fabric on his chest and crossing his arms to hold it in place, burying his hands in his armpits, until his shivers subside. Luke and Barry take turns shrugging in and out of the coat at fifteen-minute intervals, each absorbing the warmth of the other.

Rose and her father drive through a thick pea soup of fog. The car penetrates the wall of wet smoke, despite Rose's doubts. It's the kind of wet that chills you for days. They crawl forward, Rose imagining the white line at the road's edge, her father's eyes straining to pick out figures that might appear before them. On and on they inch, while the men curse their own foolishness as they cross to the other side, giving up any hope of flagging down a stranger on a night like this, wishing for a road sign that will tell them something. On the left, walking toward traffic, they see the headlights coming. Her father catches a glimpse of them.

There they are, Rose.

Rose's heart jumps as she pulls to a stop on the shoulder of the highway. She exhales the breath she's been holding in her chest, her eyes welling with relief. Her father heaves open the single heavy door on the passenger side and leans forward to allow the seatback to fold ahead and let the men squeeze in, refusing to step out into the cold dampness to give them access to the back seat, as he grumbles at them.

Get in, ye foolish shaggers.

Luke slips the coat off and hands it to Barry, then wedges himself behind Rose's father.

I told Barry you'd come looking for me, Rose. I knew you'd come.

Tall

Rose and her father think Luke is wrong about his height; maybe he's forgotten or maybe he was last measured when he was a boy. Her father brings out his measuring tape, which has lain dormant in a tool box for many years. Luke removes his shoes and stands straight against the door frame, feet together and heels touching the wall. Five eight and a half. Rose and her father laugh in a way that suggests the tape measure is wrong too.

Luke's dark curly hair has started to recede, two semi-circles carving themselves either side of his forehead. He is not the type to bulk up at the gym. The closest he came to exercise was when he went running once with his brothers, weekend athletes, and vomited on the last mile but still kept pace. Rose wonders if Luke was afflicted with Bell's palsy as a teenager and if a trace of the symptoms can linger, because of that arch in his mouth and the tiny droop in his left eye, which also happens to be somewhat lazy. Rose figures that the lazy eye affects his depth perception, which is why he finds her so attractive—he thinks I'm a nice width and kind of flat, she likes to joke. The handsomest man.

Along with baked ham and lemon pie, Luke loves the water. He is a natural at things like math, but he sometimes embarrasses Rose when he slips up and uses the wrong word for something. He told a joke among a crowd once, whose punchline should have been awesome for the guy named Johnny, who in Luke's telling, had a great *organism*.

A month after they met, Rose bought Luke a gold chain with an anchor pendant for his birthday and gave it to him early because she couldn't wait. He didn't know what to say when she handed him the little vinyl box. He wore it every day and bought a new chain for the anchor after the boys broke it roughhousing at his bachelor party. Truth be told, Luke was likely the instigator of the roughhousing. He used to walk into his mother's kitchen, lift her into his arms, turn her upside down, and shake her till loose change fell from her pockets. He'd stand her gently back on her feet with a "thanks, Mudder" and head down to the shop for a Pepsi.

Luke takes to Rose's kids like they're his own and brings his eight-year-old son, Nate, to visit on weekends. He lies on his belly on the floor for hours while Liam runs Dinkies over his back and Maggie fastens hair buckles among his curls. He watches *Road to Avonlea* and Steve Urkel with them on Sundays. And eventually when Emily comes along he is smitten. Head. Over. Heels. He hasn't held a baby in years, but he tries his hand at diapers and lays stiffly with the baby on his chest, on the couch. Luke tells Rose to go out for an hour; she can use the break and they'll be just fine.

Liam likes to wear Luke's big shoes around the house. Luke is five eight and a half but he stands taller.

Santa

Luke is sitting at the kitchen table sipping coffee after a late supper when the porch door opens a few inches and a sliver of Barry appears. His head, with its thick powdered beard, juts into the kitchen as he leans on the doorknob, a wad of tobacco in his cheek.

Where are you coming from dressed like that, now?

Just on my way down from the Manor. The seniors had their Christmas party and I did them a favour.

You didn't even need stuffing. In your glory this evening, I'm sure.

Ho, ho, ho.

Barry coughs on the last ho and Luke laughs and shakes his head at the red polyester straining across Barry's barrel chest and protruding belly. Even the fleshy nose looks the part, the broken capillaries fanning out to flushed cheeks. They chat about tomorrow morning's road trip to drop off the last load of nets for the winter.

Light footsteps patter toward the kitchen from the hallway and Liam appears in his pajamas.

Can I ge...

His words catch in his throat, and he stares at Barry in the doorway, not trusting his eyes with the spectre before him, his eyeglasses left sitting on his night table. He gapes at Barry before he pulls his gaze to Luke's face and back to Barry's, then to Luke's again. Luke winks at Liam, who comes to his senses, turns on his heel, and dashes back the way he came, thrusting himself across his room and into bed as quick as his legs can carry him. He lies on his back, straining to hear the voices through the wall, until they die away and Luke appears in his bedroom doorway. Liam is frozen in place.

You kn-know Santa?

Yes, my son, I knows Santa all to pieces.

Liam stares at Luke as if he is another apparition, wiping his eyes. He reaches toward the bedside table and slips his round-lens frames over his nose.

I can put in a good word for you with him if you promise to be good for your mother.

Liam nods his head without breaking eye contact.

Do you promise?

Yes. I promise.

Luke walks to the bed and bends to pull the covers over Liam, tucking him snugly away.

That's a good boy, then.

Liam pushes the covers away and wraps both arms around Luke's neck, hugging him.

I'll make sure Santa knows, buddy.

He rumples Liam's hair.

Good night, Liam. Sleep tight.

Good night, Luke.

Luke closes the door behind him, and Liam stares at the ceiling.

Etiquette

1992

Rose loves Christmas. Spends hours hanging balls and stringing garland, till she's happy with the perfectly aligned ornaments. The tree is the only place Rose likes symmetry. Every year she changes it. Yards of popcorn strung with needle and thread while it's still warm. Clear plastic balls that Rose bought at the craft store and filled with moss and miniature birds in hats. Personalized ornaments that say *Merry Xmas, Love Mom* with the year engraved. Now Rose pays extra to add *and Luke*. Rose lets Maggie and Liam and Nate help decorate the tree and rearranges their handiwork when they are tucked safely in bed. Nate will spend Christmas Day with his mom and come for supper.

Gifts are always boxed and wrapped in matching paper. Rose is willing to use some gift wrap with Santa faces and trains, but those papers are interspersed with ones that have stripes or snowflakes, and all the paper patterns have solid backgrounds in coordinating colours. Santa doesn't get much of the credit in Rose's house.

Rose serves turkey on her grandmother's white platter and ladles sides onto matching serving dishes. The cabbage is boiled alone in a dipper, separate from the pot of other vegetables, to keep everything clean. The potatoes are whipped.

Creamery butter, salt, milk. Pease pudding is peppered, buttered, and mashed. Carrots, turnip, and parsnip on a single platter. Cabbage alone. Gravy in boats with stands. Cranberry sauce sliced and fanned. Not a speck soils stovetop or cupboard; Rose cleans as she goes. The full platters warm in the oven until family arrives and everyone gets out of their boots. Her father's eyeglasses steam as the kitchen heat hits them, and Rose hugs him before wiping his lenses with the hem of her apron. Christmas is Rose's favourite time of the year.

Rose seats Luke at the head of the table.

Oh, she's letting me be the boss today, Granddad.

Rose's father hides his laugh with a cough.

Would you mind saying grace before we start, saucy-face.

Luke bows his head. Then, before he begins, an explosion of gas erupts from beneath the table.

Luke! For Chrissake!

Liam's head swivels from his mother's face to Luke's, and back. His eyes are saucers behind his glasses.

What makes you think it was me, hun?

Because no one else would do it! I'm mad, Luke. It's not funny.

Luke looks at Maggie and Liam with a straight face.

Sorry, hun. Now guys, we need to remember that we can't fart at the dinner table. Especially on Christmas Day.

Liam concentrates his energy to his cheeks and bum, trying his best to fart, Maggie makes a mental note to hold her toots except when she's alone, and Rose prays for patience.

Slide

Rose is late finishing the last of her Christmas shopping, and really wants to get it done. She was held up at Fabricville when she came across a bolt of faux-fur zebra-print fabric that she has no use for but can't leave behind. Rose manoeuvres the entire roll into the car, its end jammed over the headrest of the passenger seat. She'll find something to do with it. In her excitement, Rose forgets to buy the Christmas fabric she went for. The roads are slippery as she pulls onto Kenmount Road, but she has to stop at Woolco, and then whatever she has, she has. Nate wants a GT Snow Racer, but his mother says to get him a snowsuit and good winter boots.

Rose chooses a navy-blue two-piece snowsuit with red patches on its elbows and knees. The patches are reinforced with a hard, flexible liner and extra padding. She gets the same for Liam, and a pink and purple one for Maggie, with white fur around the hood. Half an hour later, Rose's cart is brimming as she heads to the checkout line.

Nate opens his presents when he visits on Christmas Eve. That's the rule in Rose's house—any gifts you're given before the twenty-fifth are fair game then and there.

Cool, Dad. That'll keep me some warm. Hope it don't get mixed up with Liam's—he'd get lost in mine.

Well, I guess we'll have to put your initials on your coats—wouldn't want to go losing Liam on his mother.

Oh, Nate, I almost forgot. There's something else here for you.

Rose goes into the hallway and is back in a second with a large box wrapped in Santa Claus paper. Nate claps his hands together and rips into Santa as soon as Rose lays the box on the floor in front of him.

Dad! Ya never! Thank you, thank you.

Don't thank me, my son. You can thank Rosie for that one.

Well, I figured what's the use of a snowsuit and good winter boots if you have no slide to break your neck on. Just promise me you'll be careful, Nate, or I'll be the one in trouble with your mother.

Nate gives Rose a hug, patting her on the back like old men do.

You're a hundred, Nate. She squeezes him and kisses his head.

Rose's Pet

Not two months home from Jon's funeral, and Luke's sister tells Rose that she got the look of baby on her, as she smiles for a picture with Luke in front of the tree.

Absolutely not, think I'd know before you would if I was pregnant. Abbey jumps to her mind, and Rose's chest tightens.

Sure enough, a week later, Rose is throwing her guts up in the toilet, shooing Maggie and Liam out of the bathroom, squeaking out, Mommy's all right, between heaves. How in god's name is she going to tell Abbey?

Rose remembers when Jon was born, on her tenth birthday. That made him hers, in her childish mind. She loved him. Went to Abbey's house every day after school—even though everyone knew that the house was haunted—to look at Jon and hope that she might get to hold him. Once, when Rose was there late, she held him while Abbey slipped into her work uniform and asked Rose to go for a drive with her.

In a singsong voice, unusual for Abbey, she says, I have to go get Jay home from the Legion again, but I don't want his buddies thinking I'm nagging, so I'll pretend I need him at work. As they drive, Abbey chats to Rose from the front seat, while Rose coos to Jon in his car seat, the quietest, happiest baby in the world. Rose is happy too.

Abbey says, When we get to the beach before the Legion, remind me and I'll tell you how many miles we drove. Do you like your teacher this year?

Rose likes her teacher. Abbey knows she always likes her teacher, but she just nods in the darkness. When they leave the Legion without him, Rose reminds Abbey that she didn't tell her how many miles.

Oh sorry, I forgot.

How did you forget, Abbey?

That was just a distraction for me, Rose.

Rose remembers the sunny afternoon that Abbey let her take Jon for a stroll. She strapped him snugly in his seat and warned Rose that he was not to be taken out of the stroller. Jon had just started walking, and Abbey had managed to scrape together twenty dollars somewhere, to get the special boots he needed. The boots were ugly but would support Jon's ankles and keep them straight. Rose didn't dare unstrap his harness, but she unlaced the boots from his poor little feet and tucked them alongside him in the dark canvas seat. Jon gurgled away, twisting his head to look up and back at Rose as she hummed to herself, imagining that he was really hers and that they could walk as far as they wanted. Jon curled his chubby fingers around one of the boots and chewed on its nose. Rose was afraid he might damage it, but she didn't have the heart to make him cry, so she left him to suck on the brown leather.

Rose stumbled on a loose plank on the boardwalk, and when she looked up again, the boot was sailing through the rungs of the wooden railing, into the black water between the pilings and the trap skiff tied up alongside. Rose sees long trails of thick kelp, or eels, shooting out from the creosote logs that bolster the walkway, as she strains to watch the boot's swirling trajectory in the dark water. Rose does not cry. Her mind races with ideas to save the boot—if she yelled to the man steering the speed boat up through the gut he might hear her and come to rescue the boot. She could jump over herself to retrieve the boot from the bottom, but how would she manage to surface? How would she keep herself afloat? Then, with wild relief, she realizes that she cannot leave the baby alone on the boardwalk; she will not be diving into the inky, dirty water today.

Her heart is heavy as she perches her arms on the rail, staring down into the water, until Jon fidgets in his seat, willing Rose's eyes to look back to his little face. *The baby is safe. That's all that matters*, she tells herself as she hoists the stroller's hind wheels into the air, and turns it back the way they came. It's a slow walk, Rose trying her best to hold Jon's gaze as he stares up at her, which is more than she manages with Abbey, when she gets back to the house.

In the following days, Abbey's husband will whisper to her that saucy Rose threw the boot overboard out of spite, and Abbey, in her grief over the loss of the boot, will let it seep in, let Jay slither between her and her little sister. Even at ten, Rose knows that she doesn't like her brother-in-law, and he dislikes her right back. Rose doesn't care as long as she gets to see Jon, but she remembers that after the boot, there are sometimes long spaces between visits.

••••• •••••• •••••

Rose, I think they are telling Abbey that Jon has a 10 per cent chance, just to prepare her.

Rose stares at Cela in the darkness of the parked car. They had spent the afternoon sitting around the living room, snorting that Jay would be forcing Jon back on his motorcycle before he even had time to heal from his accident.

No, Cela, he's eighteen. This can't happen.

Cela braces herself and barks.

Yes, Rose. It can. And I think it will. Now calm down. I need you to listen to me. I need you to help me when we go in there. And I need you to know this is happening.

I've always felt like we had a protective barrier, or something, around us, Cela.

Well we don't, Rose.

Neither of them know how long they sit in the car, quiet, before they climb their parents' steps. Rose was always afraid of motorcycles. Her fingernails hurt the warm softness of Cela's palm, as she grips tight. After a loud knock, their father opens the door in his plaid bathrobe and moccasins, and stands there, framed in the doorway, staring at his daughters. Rose blurts.

He's alive, Dad, he's still alive.

Cela and Rose spend a long night, whispering hope to their parents, until, at daybreak, the telephone rings, piercing their cocoon. Rose reaches for the receiver and brings it to her ear.

He's gone, Abbey screams into the phone, and slams it down.

****

Rose is mad at herself as she rises from her knees in the bathroom. How could she have forgotten about Abbey? Drinking wine from a paper cup in Luke's truck, like a teenager. Rose hardly noticed her father's kiss on her cheek when she and Luke came in, and his assurance that the kids were well settled on his way out. Didn't even thank him for babysitting. They tumbled into bed without brushing their teeth.

Never mind Abbey. Jon not cold in the ground, and she, like a deer in rut.

I Slept with Your Father Last Night

In the end, Rose and Cela board the plane to Alberta together, the worse for wear, not eight hours of sleep between them since Abbey called two days ago with the news. Their mother had boarded before them, wanting nothing to do with the deceit. For the best anyway, as it turned out, as they made quite a spectacle running through the gates behind the ticket agent, who decided they would be making this flight, whether they knew their own birthdays or not. The other passengers gave them little smiles of victory or threw sighs their way, depending on how aggravated they let themselves get about the ten-minute delay in leaving.

Abbey's brother-in-law, Jerry, several people ahead of them in line, had nodded and made small half waves as he wound his way to the Air Canada counter. Rose has about as much regard for Jerry as she does for his brother, Jay. Jerry is short. Balding. Brutish.

Hey, Rosie. Come. Skip through.

Then, surveying the line as he rises on his stacked heels, talking to no one in particular.

We're heading to a funeral out West.

No, no, Jerry, you go on. We're all right. I have to say goodbye to the kids anyway.

Rose had let Maggie and Liam come to the airport, against her own better judgment.

Please, Mommy, please. I promise I won't cry.

Yes, you will Maggie, my darling, you can't help yourself.

No, Mommy. I promise-promise I'll be good. I will not cry.

Rose kisses the top of each of their heads as Luke picks Maggie up, body and bones. She turns back to Cela as Luke wedges himself, Liam, and Maggie—stiff as a poker, wailing in his arms—through the sliding door. Already back to worrying whether she can pull this off, Rose wonders if the ticket agent serving Jerry has heard too much.

Please, dear sweet baby Jesus, let us get a different agent than his.

She counts the people in line, trying to determine who will fall where at the counters, sweating in her sensible layers of clothes. Cela leans in to Rose as they approach the counter of Jerry's ticket agent.

Just let me do the talking, Rose.

Rose is more than glad to let Cela handle it. Her nerves are shot already.

We'll have two standby tickets, please. Edmonton.

You know twenty-four is the age limit for purchasing a standby ticket?

Yes, we know.

Rose and Cela each have a birth certificate and a social insurance card. Not a thing this missus can do about it. What's five years anyway? They hand over the identification. The agent takes the cards and punches at the keyboard, while Rose steadies herself with her arms folded on the counter, her chin trying not to quiver. The agent glances down at a birth certificate.

When is your birthday, Ms. Donovan?

November second.

Cela steps closer and places her hand on the back of Rose's neck, rubs back and forth.

Stephanie, honey, you know your birthday is November fourth.

The agent glances at the birth certificate.

It says November fifth.

Rose puts her head in her arms to wipe the tears and snot away. Not going to get there.

Cela looks the ticket agent in the eyes.

She's just upset. She knows her birthday.

Not everyone has eight thousand dollars lying around, just waiting to be spent on two last-minute tickets to Alberta. Cela puts all her hope in the ticket agent.

Our sister's son...

You're with the gentleman in the yellow sweater? Going to his nephew's...

No. Not with him. Well... yes... same nephew.

The agent looks back to the screen.

Do you need to check bags? She hands the cards back quickly.

No. Just the carry-ons.

Good. We need to get your boarding passes done. They've finished boarding. What's the initial for Donovan, again?

Rose steps in to help out.

D.

And what's the initial for Brennan?

B.

Rose is not impressed with being grilled, but at least it appears she's getting them on this flight. The attendant grabs the passes as they print.

The doors are closing. Come with me. We'll have to run. They'll need your IDs, keep them out.

Cela grabs Rose's hand and they run full tilt through the

tiny airport behind the woman with the Air Canada badge. She rushes them through security and to the gate.

We made it. Show them your ID.

The Air Canada woman pushes the boarding passes in front of the gate attendant and waves Cela and Rose to the jetway.

Go! Good luck.

As they run the last few feet, Rose glances back and waves.

She is breathless as they board the airplane together, and Cela gives her hand a squeeze before she finally lets go. When they have taxied down the runway and are well into their ascent and levelling off, Cela looks at Rose, her hands clenched onto the armrests.

Rose, I thought you had us finished when you gave the wrong initials for the names. We're *M* and *S*. Marilyn and Stephanie. Where in god's name did you get the *B* and the *D*?

Rose looks back at Cela.

Cela, I swear to god I thought she was testing us to see if we knew the initial for the last names. Brennan and Donovan. Because I got my birthday wrong.

Cela laughs loudly, drawing another indignant stare from the woman across the aisle. They dissolve into titters like twelve-year-olds, before sinking back into their seats for the long flight, thinking about their sister Abbey.

Rose had settled the kids' things and the hamster in at Nanny and Granddad's house before they left for the airport. She had laid out a set of clothes for Maggie and Liam for each day of school while she's gone, not trusting Luke after the fiasco that time Maggie showed up at school in a flowy "skirt" that the teacher discovered had sleeves. Luke said the kids liking their outfits was more important than wearing skirts as skirts and blouses as blouses.

Rose had decided not to leave her father alone, and Luke could use the help with the kids anyway, so Maggie, Liam, and Luke would bunk out with him all week. Her heart hurt seeing her father stand by the china cabinet in the grey suede moccasins she bought for him, the fox trim clipped with blunt scissors because the flyaway fur stuck like cat hairs to his pantlegs. His head lowered and his hand resting on the cabinet's edge, to steady himself. Rose stopped to kiss his cheek and tell him she loved him before she rushed out the door. Those words rarely pass between them, but she has never left his house without leaning in and placing her lips on his cheek. And she has never left his house without feeling the unspoken words. His hand rose from the cabinet's edge to his mouth, an unconscious attempt at composure.

That's our problem sometimes, Rose, honey. We loves too much.

She hugged him and told him Luke would come straight back from the airport.

****** ****** ******

Rose's father and Luke establish a pattern. Luke dozes in bed, while her father sits in the living room, watching his shows, late into the night. When it's bedtime, he rouses Luke, who moves to the couch to settle in until after daylight, when they both get up to get Maggie and Liam off to school. Rose's father makes them a breakfast of milk and buttery toast piled high, while Luke wrestles with ponytails and tucked shirts and brushing of teeth. Granddad doesn't know why youngsters don't like warm milk anymore.

On the third night, Rose's father decides it's not sensible to be hauling Luke up out of his sleep every night.

You can stay in the bed, Luke. Only foolishness for you to be sleeping on the couch.

No b'y, that's all right, I don't mind it one bit.

Luke imagines the night he'd have, trying not to roll into his father-in-law's back, in the old water bed.

Suit yourself.

On the fifth night, Rose's father gives Luke the heads up before ducking into the bathroom.

On my way in a few minutes, Luke, wake up.

Luke half wakes, then dozes off again before John finally comes to bed.

Luke. Get up if you're getting.

No answer. *Ah well*, John thinks, as he slips his feet out of the moccasins, using his right toe to push the slipper down over his left heel. He slides his suspenders down his shoulders, unbuttons his shirt, and drapes it across the back of a chair, his belly big and round and hard. The suspenders dangle from charcoal-coloured Haggar dress pants that Abbey sent him, as he lays them across the shirt. Finally, he kicks out of his socks, leaving them bunched into balls on the floor. He sits on the navy, polyester velvet side-rail of the bed, his cotton boxers reaching halfway to his knees. He lowers himself into the waterbed like a scuba diver easing himself over the side of a boat, back first, the water in the bed's bladder rising around him as he settles down and down. Luke shifts in his sleep, absorbing the ripples as John's body displaces the water, but he does not wake.

When Rose makes her daily call in the morning, Luke grins into the phone, the right side of his mouth rising higher than the left.

Guess who I slept with last night, hun.

Snowflake

Rose is sitting on the edge of Maggie's bed, tucking the pink patchwork under her chin, while her little hands dart out from under the quilt again and reach for her mother.

There's a big girl, now. You can fall asleep without Mommy lying down with you this once, can't you?

Rose is wearing a black sequined dress and heels, her bump barely showing. They don't get a night out very often, and she's hoping to stay at the wedding until their friends are carried out of the hall on the men's shoulders. But Maggie doesn't sleep without her mother.

I don't want you to go.

Yes, darling, but Mommy and Luke will be home before you know it.

Will you come kiss me again when you get home? Will I still be awake?

I'll come kiss you. I promise.

Luke pokes his head around the corner of the half-open door, and immediately the hamster's cage falls into his line of vision. He half whispers at Rose.

Uh-oh. Hun, the hamster's dead, I think.

Maggie sits straight up in bed.

Snowflake!

56

Rose stares at Luke and speaks in a soothing voice.

No, no. The hamster is just sleeping.

No hun, I think he's dead.

Rose holds Luke's gaze and switches to an insistent sing-song voice.

No, Luke, the hamster is not dead. The hamster is asleep. Of course it's asleep. Like all good little girls.

Luke looks at Rose as if she's lost her mind, pushes the bedroom door open, reaches the cage in two strides. He eases his big hand through the tiny door, picks the hamster up by his nubby tail, and takes it from the cage. He raises his hand to eye level and shakes the hamster as if he's ringing a child-sized bell.

Look, hun, I told you. It's dead.

Maggie looks from the hamster to Rose and her face crumples. Rose heaves a loud sigh in Luke's direction as she pushes off her shoes and lies beside Maggie in the single bed, cuddling their heads together on the pillow.

I'm sorry, Maggie.

Rose shoos Luke out the door and he closes it gently. He grabs the ends of the unknotted necktie dangling on each side of his chest as he heads to the living room and folds into a chair to wait. Luke shakes his head. He hopes Rose gets Maggie to sleep.

Odds

Rose is behind the wheel of the Camaro, hugging the centre of the road to straighten out the curves to Bay Bulls, while Luke sits in the passenger seat and banters with Barry in the back. They communicate in low grunts and hand gestures, lost in the insular language of fishing and the water.

Rose nods toward Barry's nose, which is redder than usual.

Looks like you're coming down with something, Barry.

Yes, Rose, my dear, I'm half-smothered all week.

Hope you don't make my man sick while you're out there.

Luke winks at Rose and turns to look directly at Barry's hulk crammed in the back seat of the two-door vehicle.

Oh, I'll heave him overboard if he even sneezes in my direction.

Hmph, you wish.

The last few minutes pass in friendly silence, punctuated by sniffs from the back seat, until the car pulls onto the community wharf. Luke stretches as he rises out of the car, then pulls the seatback ahead and reaches his hand toward Barry, who grasps it and hoists himself forward, tumbling out into the cold morning air. They offload their bags onto planks that are scarred with engine oil and fish offal. Rose pushes open her door and steps out, as Luke saunters around the car and wraps her in his arms, kissing the top of her head. She leans close, absorbing his heat, feeling the chill in the air all the more for it.

Okay, hun, off you go. Take your time driving.

I will. Have a safe trip. Love you.

Ditto.

He heard that in a movie. Rose misses him saying *I love you* but he thinks he sounds like Patrick Swayze so she leaves it. She climbs back into the car and pulls the heavy door closed. The men heft their bags onto their shoulders as they amble toward the longliner. She revs the engine and Luke blows a kiss over his shoulder. Rose touches her hand to her mouth, then releases it. She makes a tight U-turn, easing the car off the edge of the wharf, back onto the winding road.

In the hour that the men spend in final preparation—loading groceries, securing nets, reviewing weather forecasts, and checking fluid levels and gauges—Barry protests that he shouldn't be going out on the water when he's this sick.

Luke wonders if the extra pair of hands will be worth listening to Barry complain for nine or ten days. While he jokes about heaving him over, Luke is the best one aboard to manage Barry with a grain of salt and an arch of his lip. It's no coincidence that Luke is the one who bunks with him.

A coincidence is a remarkable event with no apparent cause. When studied closely, it is actually inevitable and less extraordinary than it appears—predictable in its unpredictability. Luke says Barry is a magnet for coincidences. Luke glances at him and decides that it's not worth it.

If you're feeling too miserable to go, you really should stay home out of it.

I think I will, Luke b'y. Can't seem to shake this feeling.

All right then. You're better off. We'll see you when we land.

Barry stands on the pocked wharf with hands lazing in the pockets of his navy work pants, his green logans squelching on the dock. He watches Luke and the others grapple with securing wooden boxes and the dory as seagulls shriek obscenities above his head. When they're ready to cast off, Barry unties the *Elizabeth Coates* from the bollard and tosses the bow line to Luke as Ed and Wayne tamp the last hatch in place, and Gerald heads into the wheelhouse with the skipper, Pat Coates. Luke extends both hands as the coiled rope unwinds in the air, landing haphazardly at his feet. He grabs the frayed end of thick yellow nylon and raises his hand in a wave to Barry, before turning away.

Sea Over Bow

1994

Rose supposes this is how it happened. They were on their way in from the Grand Banks in a boat that should never've seen the banks, pushed along by a storm straight out of the history books. The waves rose up to their full height—or a rogue wave maybe—fifty-five feet high, charging at them. And they sitting there—or lying in their bunks down forward—in a fifty-foot boat that should never've seen the banks. Anyone who knows anything about physics—which Rose doesn't—knows that a boat can only withstand waves up to its own length. Fifty-five foot waves.

Rose got up late in the night to answer the phone.

Hello.

Hello? Rose? It's Peggy. Peggy Coates.

Oh. Hi, Peggy. How are you?

Good, my dear. Luke asked me to give you a call because the reception is bad on the radio. I hardly heard a word Pat said. They're making decent time now though. They'll be landing at six in the morning.

It's the only time Luke didn't call Rose himself. They haven't spoken since she left him at the wharf nine days ago. Him and Barry, who had the good sense to develop a flu before they untied and was left standing on the wharf to find his own way home. Luke always calls Rose on the way in.

Rose's father called her over and over in the three days before they were due.

Did you hear from Luke yet?

Did he call?

Did you hear from him yet?

Like a metronome.

On the morning she is going for him, Rose's parents are getting Maggie and Liam off to school and taking care of the baby, 'til Rose and Luke get home. She doesn't know what she'll do without them right around the corner anymore, when she moves into her new house.

Rose spent way too long in the shower, thinking about Luke until the water ran cold, and she's running way behind. They'll be landing by now and Rose has over an hour's drive, if she ever gets out the door.

When Luke calls, tell him I'll be there by seven thirty.

It's raining, and Rose is driving fast. She decides to stop and get a little lunch for Luke at the gas station. It'll make him smile, that lopsided smile. The five minutes it takes will be worth it. He probably ran out of Pepsi days ago. Rose arrives at the wharf but they're not in yet. It's seven thirty. She pulls out onto the head of the wharf. Sits there. Drives up the hill. Back down again to the wharf. Up the hill again. Pacing back and forth on the narrow road. At nine thirty she calls Peggy from the pay phone in the porch of the IGA.

Why didn't you call me before you went out there, to see if I'd heard from them?

You said they'd be in by six.

Well, my dear, I never goes out 'til I hears from Pat.

Luke usually just calls me the night before.

Why don't you go to the office and see if Bud's heard from them?

Rose doesn't know Bud from Adam and has no interest in checking with him for messages from Luke. Up the coiled road to the top of the hill again. She parks on a point to watch the harbour. When she spots them, it will still be forty minutes or so before they land. *Shit*, Rose thinks. *Why didn't Luke let me know he'd be late?* So she drinks the Pepsi she bought him and she eats his orange Aero bar.

Winds down the hill again. Back to the IGA to call her mother to tell her she's going to the plant to wait for Luke. They'll be late getting back. Her mother will get lunch for Maggie and Liam. But they're expecting Rose and Luke to be home.

Up the hill again to the point to watch. The rain beats a worried refrain on the windshield.

Rose sings along, Take my hand, precious Lord. She wonders what made her think of that song.

She finally goes to the office to speak to Bud at ten thirty, because she can't sit all day watching an empty harbour. Rose opens the door to the fish plant, assaulted by the smell of fish guts and booming echoes of the building that are second nature to Luke. She asks a group of men where the office is, walks up the narrow stairs, crosses the large room to the desk, asks to speak to Bud Byrne. The secretary takes her name. She disappears and out he comes. He isn't a bit surprised to find a wife, who he's never laid eyes on before, standing in the plant office.

I'm Rose.

Rose. Nice to meet you. Don't go worrying now about the boys. I'm not even concerned. Coates is a seasoned fisherman. Wouldn't be out there if he didn't think he could handle it.

Rose nods along as he talks.

Do you want a cup of tea?

She follows him to the kitchen where he leaves her and sends the secretary to serve tea. People come and go. Small talk. Quiet. Then an old man comes in and sits down, introduces himself—he used to run the plant before he turned it over to his son.

So who are you, now?

Rose. Rose Tremblett. Luke Tremblett's wife.

No glimmer of recognition.

He fishes with Pat Coates.

The old man looks her up and down in her chair.

Well my dear, you better get down on your knees and start praying to Jesus if your husband is out there in this with Pat Coates.

The radio is turned off. There is no window in the kitchen.

When her cup is empty, Rose's mother calls.

Cela is coming out to wait with you.

Why?

No reason. Just don't want you sitting there all day by yourself.

Pat Coates's son comes and goes. At twelve o'clock Rose goes back out to the office to see Bud again.

Oh, I'm not too concerned. If it was anyone else I would be, but Pat...

Rose tries to focus on his face when she realizes he's still talking.

If they're not in by five o'clock, I'll start to worry.

Rose wipes her nose on her fist.

If they're not in by five, I'll be in the mental.

Cela had woken early, before daylight, and Luke was the first thing on her mind. After hours of waiting, she went to Bay Bulls to sit with Rose.

Rose's mother and father were still at the house waiting, when Maggie and Liam got home from school. Many of the crew's family and friends gathered at the Lighthouse Lounge by the lift bridge across the gut and whittled the day away together. The bridge did not cease its rise and fall, its methodical releasing of boats into the bay under its tutelage and gathering them back again.

At five thirty, Cela and Rose leave the fish plant for the drive to Cela's house in St. John's, to wait for Luke. Someone brings Maggie, Liam, and Emily to Cela's. Rose and Cela stay up all night, huddled together on the couch. The baby swaddled at Rose's feet in her chair, its fabric a cheerful print of white puffy clouds in blue sky. Rose and the kids call the chair the *baby's cloud*. Between phone calls to Abbey, they talk, tell stories, make each other laugh. Between watching the rain pelting the picture window, staring out into the impenetrable black, and startled jumps every time the phone rings.

Rose spends three parts of the night getting second-hand news. And standing in the window praying that Luke isn't freezing. Then standing in the window, praying that Luke is freezing. She'll warm him when he comes. And at five o'clock in the morning, Rose gets sick of it. So she calls the Coast Guard herself. And she talks to someone named George.

Immortal

1994

Rose has to tell the kids that he's gone. Maggie and Liam in the one bed. Still in their clothes. She put them to bed still dressed. In a little single bed in Cela's basement. So they wouldn't be kept awake all night. Two of them lying together. Rose teetering on the edge of the bed.

Guys, we think Lukey is gone.

Liam looks at Rose then turns away. The quietest thing.

Young people are immortal. They lose their immortality one of two ways. Either quickly, by dying, or slowly, by living, mortality growing heavier by the year. Luke and Rose were immortal when they met, enough life under their belts to know they wanted better, enough life left to get it if they were serious about it. They were serious. They made love two nights after they met and then wondered why they waited so long. Luke gave up drinking and Rose settled down and they made it.

Luke and Rose were building a house. The day they started, Luke pegged the perimeter and dug holes for the foundation, which he would fill with cement pylons poured into fibreboard forms. When Rose surveyed his progress that first day, the grass was still thigh-high, except where Luke had tamped it down with his footprints, and she couldn't imagine their house growing within the twine outline. It was too much to take in. As Rose wandered within the parameters of her home, the grass swished in the wind and the first drops of a torrential downpour hit her cheeks. The next day, Rose cried because a mouse had drowned in one of the rain-filled holes overnight.

When Luke wasn't on the boat, he was at their house. It was late summer before the second floor was added and he would hoist Liam up the ladder to see his bedroom. Maggie was afraid of heights and decided she'd wait for a staircase. She satisfied herself by sitting on the rough wood floor of their living room and peering up through the spaces in the ceiling, catching glimpses of Liam as he ran between what would be their bedrooms. By the time they finished with the fish for the year, Luke should be ready for windows and doors.

Rose was anxious to get the fishing season over with. They made the last trip for the fall in the *Elizabeth Coates*, to the Grand Banks, where they hadn't yet ventured in this boat. Coates intended to have her fibreglassed over the winter to make her more suitable for chasing the fish farther out. They were hoping for a couple tuna to recoup the losses on the coast of Labrador, where half their gear was destroyed in a storm. But the trip to the banks was disappointing too. They were heading home with six thousand pounds of turbot and two leftover tuna tags. For days before they'd left for the banks, Luke wondered if he should bother to go. All it would have taken was one word from Rose and he'd have stayed home. She kept her mouth shut.

Now Rose has to tell the kids that he's gone. Liam had just started calling him Dad.

Maggie and Liam are in the one bed.

Guys, we think Lukey is gone.

Liam looking at Rose then turning away. The quietest thing.

Record

1994

Rose sits in her parents' living room and waits for the police officer to arrive. She understands this is standard procedure and it won't take long. Rose is in no hurry. She has nowhere, really, to be. The baby is sleeping, and Maggie and Liam are here in the middle of it all. All of this mayhem. This adult upset that they watch without anyone explaining.

The policeman is escorted into the living room. Rose rises and shakes his hand. He introduces himself and mumbles something about her troubles. Rose sinks back onto the couch, knowing he doesn't expect chit-chat or tea. He is not company.

Do you mind if I ask you a few questions... Rose.

No, that's fine.

Thank you. I guess we'll start by asking if your husband had... has any identifying marks.

What do you mean?

I mean like birthmarks. Or scars. Tattoos.

Oh. Well. He has a tiny dark spot on his lower left side. Hardly big enough for a stranger to notice though. His mouth droops a little when he smiles.

The young police officer shifts in his seat, touches the pulse in his temple.

Scars. Tattoos.

Yes. He has four tattoos. On his arms.

Can you tell me about them?

He has one on each of his upper arms and two on his forearms.

Rose and the officer sit looking at each other. Rose turns the questions over. The answers. It feels like she is doing something. Like she's contributing.

The officer looks down at his notepad and draws.

Can you describe the tattoos?

He has one that says *Mom*. In a heart.

And where is that located?

On his left arm. Up here.

Rose feels like an actor. This is not real. She's part of a search party looking for a missing person, combing through underbrush for signs that they passed this way.

Okay, good. What else?

He has one that says *Death Before Dishonour*. With a skull. On his right arm. Down here.

Oh. Was he in the Marine Corps?

No. Why?

It's their emblem. I just thought…

No. He was never in the armed forces.

That's fine.

He has one that says *Charlene*. In a ribbon. On his upper right arm. I colour that one in with black pen sometimes.

The police officer scribbles in his notepad again. He writes *Charlene* in small letters.

Please tell me about the last one.

Homeward Bound. With a ship. On his lower left arm.

The officer does not look up.

Does he have a dentist? Would he have dental records?

I've never seen him have so much as a toothache. His teeth are good. Yes, I'm sure he'd have dental records. Dr. Greene.

The policeman rises from his chair a little more abruptly than Rose would expect for a man discussing dental records. Identifying marks. He is anxious to be gone, Rose notices now. Restless to get back to his office, to log details of tattoos and dental records that may come in handy. Paperwork.

Rose understands the policeman's need to be useful. His rush to get out of the room she's sitting in, to get to the dentist's office. In case one of the bodies washes up from fifty miles offshore, so bloated by the time it reaches home that dental records will be the only way of knowing which of the men has shown up. The policeman will have everything in hand. Rose understands.

Rose wants Luke to know that she misses him already. Every action is carefully orchestrated to show it. She walks slowly through the drag of heavy air in every room she enters, her muscles and her sinew and her bones participating in the protest. She draped herself over Luke's car in his parent's driveway—was that only two days ago—stroking the warm bonnet, and noticed the neighbours watching.

Sat in Luke's passenger seat, Cela at the wheel, stopping in the lineup of cars, waiting for the fishing boats to pass under the lift bridge, so they could head back home. Sat in the passenger seat behind a lineup of cars, exposed. Feeling like the car was transparent and everyone—walking by with their hoods tied tight against the wind, or glancing in rear-view mirrors as salt water sprayed over their windshields, or raising corners of lace to look out their kitchen windows—could see Rose's toes clenched inside her socks, her heart clenched inside her coat. She prayed that Barry's wife wouldn't push her curtain aside and see Rose, see that she knows Barry is still alive.

Rose doesn't know the things she will learn, that lie dormant for now, while she goes through the motions. She only knows that Luke is gone and she is longing for him already. As indelibly as if it were carved into her skin.

Compensation

Rose doesn't know what the rush is, for the man from Worker's. She wants to tell him they're not cold in their graves yet. But she supposes they are. Rose sits at Bee's kitchen table for the meeting. The man from Worker's thanks Bee for hosting these wives at her house, saving him multiple meetings to deliver the same information. The other two women, in different towns, he will meet with separately. Rose sits beside Trish, across from Bee and the man. The women attempt small talk, but they don't really know each other, and no one has slept in days. There's not a trivial thought among them.

The man is here to walk them through the process; he rustles the documents and forms he's brought for the women. They watch him as he talks, not absorbing a single word; he shuffles his papers again. Trying to get them to focus is useless. Easier to just run through his spiel, then fill out the forms himself and have the wives sign. They lay their husbands' birth certificates and social insurance cards on the table in front of him, each in their turn, like children. He wishes he could go outside for a draw.

When the man packs his things into his briefcase and shakes each of their hands, the women sit still at the table and watch through the window as he leaves. They glance at each other, fish for words to share. The women breathe their husband's names, forgetting to use past tense.

Bee says, Me and Ed might have our rows, but if he was here now, he'd know he was loved.

Bee is tall and substantial and hates her thick ankles. She inhales deeply, then exhales.

He'd know he was loved.

It's the first time Rose has been inside Bee's house. She's turned the car around in the driveway of the pale mint saltbox a couple of times, dropping Ed off after a trip.

***** ***** *****

Run me on down the hill now, Rose, like the good woman you are.

Where to, Ed?

The shop.

Ed looks as salty as they come, with his ruddy complexion, hardened by the ocean air, but his ginger blond hair and perpetual grin round the rough edges.

You can go on, Rose. I'll walk back up the hill.

Don't be so silly, Ed. I don't mind waiting.

God bless ya, my darling, if you believes in 'im. I'll just be a minute.

The bell on the glass door jingles as Ed pushes his way back out, a half-dozen Black Horse under his left arm, a gaggle of small brown paper bags clutched in his right hand.

He squeezes into the back seat of the Camaro, behind Luke.

Candy. For the neighbourhood youngsters. There's a hundred up on the hill, like gulls. They expects it now. Some vexed if I came back without it.

He chuckles and hugs the beer case close to his body on the back seat.

Ed eases himself out of the car, ducking under the belt

73

strap, then tucks his head back in, for the beer, and gives a wink. When he straightens to his full height and strolls away toward his house, his blue plaid flannel jacket catches the children's eyes, and they flock to him, squawking.

············

Rose shifts in her wooden chair, looks Bee in the eye.

Yes, Bee girl, I'm sure Ed knows that he's loved.

Rhyme

My father went to sea, sea, sea
To see what he could see, see, see
But all that he could see, see, see
Was the bottom of the bright blue sea, sea, sea

Oh, Helen had a steamboat
The steamboat had a bell
When Helen went to heaven
The steamboat went to
Hello, operator
Please give me number nine
And if the line is busy
I'll kick you from
Behind the old piano
There was a piece of glass
And Helen slipped upon it
And broke her little
Ask me no more questions
I'll tell you no more lies

And if you don't believe me
I'll punch you in the...

Rose's eyes stare past Maggie as she pictures the gravel-topped school grounds from when she was Maggie's age, as if she is still there, and her ears flood with the chorus of childhood ditties, chanted like war cries over the teacher's clanging bell. She is reading aloud from the little baggie book lying open in her lap, the short phrases rising off the paper like an incantation — *the bottom of the sea, is a lovely place to be* — lulling Maggie into rapt attention as she nestles beside her mother on the couch. A baggie book — because it is for primary readers and fits in a plastic Ziploc bag — is small, lightweight, and colourful, with few words and knockout graphics to keep the child's attention (all the better to make good readers of them, my dear). Rose imagines the teacher filling the baggies, which are labelled with names as pretty as the pages themselves — Maggie and Mollie and Sheila — methodically removing and replacing soft-covered booklets each day like an assembly-line worker, so accustomed to the rhythmic repetition that she can do it without thinking. The easiest part of her day. The teacher doesn't stop to think about the book she slips into Maggie's bag.

The colourful shapes on the page swarm in Rose's vision. Treasure troves of fish, sea shells, pirate chests, all brimming with turquoises, blues, and greens that look as though they are shot through with light, purples and golds to rival a king's robe, yellows the colour of sunbursts and lemon peels. The pages look backlit, a halo effect over everything. A deep-sea diver — in a beige and brown suit, childlike, helmet with an iron cage over the glass front — is suspended at the heart of the action, dull against the vibrant backdrop, tubes and hoses snaking up beyond the edge of the page.

The fishes swim past, having a blast. Rose is back in the school-yard, chanting, chanting. Clapping games were as important a part of play for Rose as they are for Maggie, absorbing the culture of the playground, the mockery and subversive nature of some of the rhymes. Watching the older children, making friends, learning about life. The lineup waiting to go back into school after recess can often be made shorter by clapping and chanting.

Rose finishes reading to Maggie — *the oysters are girls, for they're wearing pearls* — turns the last page, and closes the tiny book.

Here darling, pass Mommy the baggie. I'll sign the paper so Miss knows that I read your story for you.

Rose slips the book back into the Ziploc bag and turns to Emily, who is propped on pillows on the couch, beside Maggie. Rose claps her hands close to the baby's face and Emily blinks, before Rose takes her in her arms to feed. As the baby sucks, Rose rocks back and forth, back and forth.

And your daddy's at the bottom of the sea, sea, sea,

And your daddy's at the bottom of the sea.

Tree

1995

Rose walks in the back door of their rental with her grocery bags, piles them on the counter, and heads through the kitchen into the living room, where Cela is watching *Rugrats* with the kids, balancing Emily on her knee. Rose feels like something is different. The Christmas tree is missing.

Love of Christ! Who did that now? Haven't even got a picture of the youngsters in front of it yet.

Cela scoops Emily into her arms and stands.

February's over Rose. You said you'd take it down in February.

I know February's over. Who took down the goddamn tree?

Mom came over and did it.

Well, Mom had no business. Did she take a picture?

She was only being helpful, Rose.

She thought she was.

We can get a picture.

Okay.

Cela pulls on her boots and a sweater, traipses out the front door, around the side of the house through snow halfway to her knees, grasps the tail end of the dead tree, drags it back around and in through the door again; it is curled inward on itself, scraps of tinsel clinging to the arthritic branches as it is forced through the doorway arse foremost, dry needles abandoning ship and scattering to the far corners of the hallway.

There. We'll set it up and snap away.

Thank you, Cela. We can just decorate the bottom and sit them on the floor.

Cela sets the tree back in the green metal stand in the corner and tightens the screws. Rose rifles through dog-eared cardboard boxes and adds some homemade ornaments and a string of red plastic beads to the lower branches, while Maggie changes into her dark green crushed-velvet lounge pants and tunic, and Liam voices an objection to the debacle before him that falls on deaf ears. Maggie strolls back into the living room clasping a gold chain-link belt around her waist, sits in front of the partially decorated tree, and scoops Emily into her lap on the floor. She is glad she gets to wear her Christmas suit again. Rose cajoles Liam to join in the effort, and he finally scoots a little plastic yellow chair in front of the tree and plops down in his T-shirt and sweatpants. The frame of the camera captures Maggie smiling straight into it, Emily bouncing in her sister's arms, a few leftovers from months ago hanging on the bottom quarter of a very dead tree, and Liam slouched in his seat trying to sit still, tears streaming out from under his round lenses.

All right, my babies. Let's have some ice cream.

Rose exhales as she rises from her crouch.

Origami

1996

The goal is to transform a flat, square sheet of paper into an art piece, through folding and sculpting techniques, without cutting, gluing, or marking the paper. The principles of origami are used in life-saving engineering applications like stents, but it originated as a form of recreation and entertainment, a soothing distraction for the fingers and the mind.

Rose buys a children's book with step-by-step instructions and brightly patterned papers, but she abandons it in frustration, swearing under her breath. The best she can do is the paper planes and boats she's made her whole life. Emily and Rose fold the sheets of paper together in simple lines and Emily laughs when Rose's airplane soars over her head. Rose fills a mixing bowl with water, the paper boats tipping on their sides as Emily tries to blow them across the surface like her mother. By two years old, Emily is the glue that holds the family together, distracting Rose from the turmoil she feels. Emily has been moulded by things outside her mother's control since she lay in a Moses basket on her father's empty side of the bed.

Rose had their home finished. She felt driven to see the last nail hammered into the house that Luke built, to live there with her children. She feels there is something there for her. A customer of Rose's, a retired carpenter who was widowed and had remarried a young mother with two kids, offered to finish the house for Rose for free, so she hired him and paid him to do it, and Luke's brothers helped with the work.

Rose and her kids went out West to Alberta to visit Abbey the summer after Luke died, but they flew home early because Rose could not miss the first strip of siding being attached, underneath the windows, spanning the width of the front porch. The windows were tall, running from the ceiling to about a foot above the floor.

On Christmas Eve, Rose decorated a small artificial tree and they spread sleeping bags on the unfinished living-room floor, the drywall not yet skimmed with plaster, Emily poking her tiny fingers into the seams of the uneven edges. Luke's family and friends all came to visit and drank beer and strummed guitars and danced in the family room and the kitchen.

Rose and the kids moved into the completed house in the spring, before Emily turned two. Luke's family and friends came again to help with the move, flowered couches and plaid couches and a striped couch, interspersed with tables and chairs, bedroom sets and lamps, and clocks and boxes. Liam drew a picture of his furnished house for school, and Mrs. O'Keefe said, "Now Liam, I don't think you have five couches in your house."

When Rose did not have it in her to get everyone off to bed at night, she unfolded the sofa bed in the family room, and they all bundled together there until morning. And on the nights when they went upstairs, they slept in Rose's bed, and she lay among the kids and the blankets in darkness, staring out the window at the white eaves of the house. Sometimes, when Emily fussed while her mother was at the kitchen sink, Rose would lift her onto the countertop and allow her to run the long stretch of it, unfettered. Once, Rose found a dead mouse stuck in the door panel of the dishwasher, and Emily ran to the front door and called out for Nanny Tremblett while her mother shrieked. Emily knows Nanny can help.

Unlike newer methods, traditional Japanese origami used various shapes of paper that could be cut and glued, folding mistakes out of sight instead of tossing the whole thing in the waste bin. This is more in line with Rose's way of doing things.

Emily has a habit of toddling over to the low-slung living-room window, perching her bum on the protruding ledge, and folding her tiny body like origami to fit neatly along the window's edge. She lies the width of the window, pulls her knees up, wraps her arms around bent legs, and tucks her head to her chest. She lays there in a little ball, unmoving, until her mother notices. Sometimes, Emily pretends not to hear her mom murmur about that silly girlie and waits for the exclamation of surprise, "My goodness where has that Emmy gotten to," before hurling herself onto the floor and unfolding in a burst of giggles.

Out

1996

Cela comes in the front door and Rose is seated at the head of the oval table in the dining room, the sink behind her in the kitchen piled with dirty dishes, dried oatmeal and Kraft Dinner caked to the bowls on the table. She looks up from where she's sitting and lays down the black octagon-shaped plate that she's holding.

Oh hi, Cela. How was work?

Cela is running the salon for Rose while she's off.

Good. I got a couple free tickets for a whale-watching tour. Don can't go. I'll take you. Oh, and Mrs. Brent went through the coffee table.

What?

Planked herself on the edge of the glass top to gossip with Mrs. Barrett, and I guess her bum is heavier than she thought. She leaned back and next thing you know, she's legs up.

Oh, my god!

Yep. You know the bar running under the middle of the glass—stuck between that and the edge of the table. Looked like a turtle flipped on its back. Little arms and legs flailing. She wails, "Cela, help me," and we laughed so hard at the poor soul we couldn't get her out.

Seriously.

Swear to god. Then when we all got calmed down enough to get her out and get the glass swept up, I brought Mrs. Barrett in to shampoo her hair. Had her back in the chair, leaned right in over her. Meek and mild she looks up at me and says, "Mike'll be a month picking glass out of her arse." Girl, I almost died.

Cela puts the kettle on to boil and Rose picks up the dinner plate again, scraping it into the garbage bin that sits directly in front of her under the table's edge. When she has the plate scraped clean of food, she lays it carefully into the trash can, reaches to pick up another, scrapes its contents into the bin, then lays that plate on top of the last in the garbage can.

What in the name of god are you doing?

Throwing out my dishes.

But why?

Because I don't want to wash them, Cela.

Cela looks her in the eye, holding her gaze.

Rose, girl, it's time to start thinking about getting back to work or something. We need to start getting you out and about.

Cela sits on the chair next to Rose, scoots it close, and holds Rose's hand. They sit quietly, staring at the discarded food in the garbage bin, and the plates, neatly scraped and stacked beside it among the trash.

It's almost two years, Rose honey. You need to get yourself out of the goddamn house.

Iceberg

What is time? A unit of measure? In the same way that an inch is a unit of measure? What is it measuring? Is it an event? A dimension? A container? Can you describe it? How does it act? Does it move? Flow? Pass?

Time has no preconceived notions of you, no expectations. It doesn't care if you discover its secrets. It does not care if you shed it like old skin. You will spend your life contained by something that is not a container, measured by something not measureable, defined by something indefinable. Or you can lay it aside. You can slip outside of it, walk around it, move backward and forward through it.

Think of time, as you know it, as the tip of the iceberg. There is so much more. Hidden beneath the surface. Lean over. Put your face close. Look in.

****** ***** *****

A piece of time, dislodged, floats down from Arctic iciness, through latitudes that soften it and make it come undone. It catches the breath in your ribcage, sweeps away every vestige of your old ways of thinking about white, reconfigures neural pathways. Here is a white that makes you shiver.

The iceberg in the distance is older than Jesus — in fact, two thousand years of ice has melted off its surface since it began its slow drift south. Rose and Cela are heading out through The Narrows to see it, aboard a tour boat operated by a man who met Luke once. It is a sunny summer day and they pose for pictures in their T-shirts, looking for all the world like tourists in their sunglasses and matching open-mouthed smiles, a Rubik's cube of houses clinging to the cliffs in the background.

The tide is high so the longliner steers around Chain Rock and steams away from the berg toward Quidi Vidi, Rose imagining the boom that stretched across the harbour to keep submarines out during wartime. Whole worlds exist beneath waves that crash against rocks in high-spirited succession, each as different as a fingerprint. The boat's engine drones as the skipper slows her and eases in through The Gut. Rose thinks she could touch the shiny grey-green rocks to port and starboard if she leaned far enough over the rail. They circle The Gut's circumference, their eyes devouring new, glass-walled houses that rub shoulders with fish shacks whose clapboard siding barely remembers red paint, hands waving from stageheads and front steps of houses fashioned on pilings that plunge into fathoms of impenetrable black. Icebergs have been known to ground themselves here, blocking The Gut's entrance, causing headaches for fishermen and havoc for the tour operators, until high winds and rough seas coerce them into breaking up, rolling over, or moving on their way, leaving behind pieces of time and gouges in the ocean bottom. The wounds on the ocean floor will still show in a thousand years.

As they head back toward the iceberg, they are greeted by whales and schools of porpoises who are ensuring that the tourists enjoy their day. Rose has spent much of her life on or around the water but has never seen it in such a playful mood, tossing its secrets up to be grabbed like brass rings. A whale breaches close enough to look Rose in the eye, then as quickly thrusts its body beneath the surface and throws its tail into the air, causing Rose to cry out, Look, look!

The skipper is pulled magnetically in circles around the shoreline by the sights, the charter filling itself up with stories of the intelligence of mammals and questions of whether that fin belongs to an angel shark or that tail is attached to a long-haired siren. When all eyes are drawn upward as an airplane turns and loops in over Signal Hill, cresting the tip of the iceberg in the distance, Rose wonders if Orville Wright is standing on The Lookout guiding the plane to its touchdown. She looks across The Battery at the fence, far away, that runs down the incline of Southside Hill, and wonders about the human insistence on compartmentalizing things—the only animal Rose can imagine being contained by the fence is a goat, and she wonders if the song about Paddy McGinty's goat was written here.

Rose repeatedly clenches and releases her hands in her lap, as the passengers snap photos of silhouettes in the sinking sun. Finally, they come within a breath of the iceberg, time immemorial creeping into the fabric of Rose's being, the iceberg's chill emanating like a light into her darkest recesses. The cold is not remote—it is more like a balm that spreads its comfort into her muscles and her sinew and her bones. She stares into the berg's multi-faceted surfaces, dances on its planes, gets lost in its crevices. Rose comes unmoored.

Totem

On October thirteenth, Rose stares out the window of the house Luke built at the late blooms in her garden, lost in the memory of two years ago. Her elbow is propped on the arm of the couch, fist under her chin. Just as her eye catches a flutter of blue-green among the white hydrangeas by the fence, the whir of colour swoops across the garden to meet her gaze, an iridescent jewel at the open window. The hummingbird's feathers catch the sun, flashes of changing hues like an oil slick on water, the air whirling as the bird hovers eye level with Rose.

Where is your joy?

Rose leans forward and whispers to the tiny bird.

I don't know what you mean.

The fluttering wings move in the pattern of an infinity symbol. Timeless. A hummingbird will travel thousands of miles when required. It seeks the sweetest nectar. A hummingbird maintains vibrational frequencies in a state of well-honed, regulated balance, instead of frittering away energy. In the world of totems, a hummingbird is a messenger and a stopper of time.

Do not waste your vitality on fear. There are no obstacles. I will return every year to allow you to seek your happiness. But it will cost you.

The bird hangs in the balance, suspended in time, watching Rose, its highly evolved visual-processing centre reading imperceptible cues, before it changes the angle of its wings and darts laterally to the window's edge, moving aside to make room for her.

Rose rises from the couch, smooths her black tunic, pulls a slender white tube from where she has it tucked into her bra and glosses her lips. She raises one leg and rests her heel on the sill, stoops low and folds herself out the window, heedless of the mesh that closes behind her as she passes through the screen. Rose follows the bird around the corner of the house, where it flutters its wings in invitation, its sinuous body passing through the windowless, two-storey wall, unhindered.

Together

Rose does an incantation — *muscle sinew bone, muscle sinew bone* — and steps through the wall into the living room. Rose feels the pull of time in the wall, knows this will age her, but she doesn't care. The same as she paid no heed when she used laxatives to purge as a teenager, against her mother's warnings that she'd be sorry when she ran into bowel trouble later, not really believing in forty at the time.

Luke is standing in the living room. Like he was expecting her.

He stretches his hands toward her as she crosses the room and fits her body to his; he's solid. Rose wraps her arms around him just below his chest, her fingers splayed on his back. She presses her nose right into the centre of his chest, where the curly hair is flattened under his sweater, taking him in until she nearly smothers, then turns her head to breathe. They stand together for a lifetime, before Luke leads her upstairs.

Rose lies on her back, right hand resting across her bare belly, stretch marks hidden under the duvet. Luke reaches over, deliberately rearranges her hand spread-eagled, one finger at a time, as if she is being fingerprinted, click, click, click, click, on her stomach. Friction of finger against finger as he slides his own the length of hers, the weight of his warm hand bearing down.

They lie easily together, legs entwined, like there is nothing else needs doing. Whispers and smiles, and cheeks cupped in hands. Low laughter and pulling of blankets, and fingers tracing spines. As the day wanes, Rose stretches to kiss Luke's temple before she eases her arm from under his sleeping body and pushes herself out of the bed, into her clothes, and down the stairs. Rose repeats the words—*muscle sinew bone*—then steps back through the living-room wall, into October.

George

Rose stares at the telephone in her hand and then raises it to her ear.

Hi, I'm calling to ask you about my husband, Luke Tremblett. He's aboard the *Elizabeth Coates*.

There is a pause at the other end of the line. The man clears his throat.

Yes, ma'am. I know who your husband is.

Okay, good. I need to talk to you then. I need you to be frank with me. I need to know what's happening. And I would appreciate it if you could just be honest. What's your first name again?

George, ma'am.

Thank you. It's five o'clock in the morning, George. I haven't slept yet. I've spent all day sitting in a fish plant and all night sitting by the phone.

Yes, ma'am, I imagine you have.

And I can't do it anymore. No one calls but Abbey. And Luke's brothers. To see how I am. To ask about the kids. To share some rumour they heard. But no one knows what's going on.

Good to have family, Mrs. Tremblett.

I'm tired of getting second-hand news, George. Do you know anything? Do you know what's going on? It was a bad night. These men are a day late George. They're missing.

Ma'am.

George clears his throat again.

They're missing aren't they, George?

Yes, ma'am, they're missing.

You know more, don't you?

Is there someone there with you, Mrs. Tremblett? You're not there alone, are you?

No, George, I am not alone. But I need you to tell me. You promised you'd be honest with me.

I did.

George exhales deeply into the receiver.

You don't have good news for me, do you, George?

No, ma'am, I do not.

I can't take it anymore.

Ma'am.

Just tell me, George. Please. Anything is better than this.

At this point, Mrs. Tremblett, the Coast Guard is conducting a salvage…operation.

Salvage.

Yes, ma'am. Salvage.

Rose turns the word over, feels it somersault in her head, ricochet off her skull like shrapnel.

What does that mean, exactly?

I'm very sorry to have to say, Mrs. Tremblett, but we do not expect to find survivors at this point. Very sorry. I can have my supervisor call you when he gets in, if you'd like.

There is silence, and Rose realizes that George has stopped speaking.

Thank you, George.

Rose sets the phone slowly back in its cradle, as if her hesitance will preserve the connection. She wishes she could go back to the seconds before she told George that anything is better. To stay there in the not knowing.

Rose stares at her hand as she hangs up the telephone.

Breathe

When she breaks through into the night air, her shoulder catching as she passes through the wall, Rose picks her way to the car parked out front, unable to bring herself to step back through her front door, to her children, yet. She pulls open the heavy door of the blue Camaro — the most ridiculous car a woman with three kids has ever driven. Luke sold his pickup truck when the moratorium started, and when his brother asked what he was getting next Luke said, "A good pair of sneakers." When he returned from Labrador, Luke got a great deal on the Chev, and now Rose is left with a two-door car, with sport rims and a car seat. She steps in and leans her forehead on the steering wheel, shivering. Sits there for a long time. Goes for a drive to settle her breathing.

When Rose gets back home, her father is sitting in the dining room, Emily snoring on his shoulder. Liam and Maggie are in Rose's bed but call out "Mommmmy" in unison as soon as they hear the door. Rose doesn't say a word, takes Emily from her father, switches off the light, heads upstairs to the bedroom and settles her beside Liam and Maggie, then crawls in herself. She stares at the ceiling, trying to doze off, her right arm across her forehead. The children lie still, waiting. Her father sits at the table in the dark.

Rose thinks about when she was Maggie's age and her mother took turns with her father getting her and Cela and Abbey off to school on winter mornings once fishing was done for the year. One stayed in bed while the other toasted homemade bread on the stovetop, turned it by slipping a butter knife under its middle and flipping it like a pancake, piled it with butter, and filled mugs with hot sugary milk. A tower of toast that the girls stretched their plates across the table for, her father serving four slices to each of them and himself, the girls hoping for slices that were not scorched. There were usually a couple of each, though her father was a little more careful than her mother to not burn the bread. Rose placed the best slice at the bottom of her stack, pulled each slice in half, ate the soft middle of the bread, and made a ring around her plate with the crusts.

She dreams about Luke making toast for Emily, the bread stacked so high it breaks through the ceiling, rising into the sky.

When she wakes, Rose pushes herself out of bed to get Liam and Maggie off to school. She supposes it is a school day. As she dresses them and brushes Maggie's long brown hair, she wonders what choices people would make if they were in control. Would a mother give up a child to save a husband? Would a child know which parent was the right one to keep? How much would any one person sacrifice? It will be a whole year before she can visit Luke again. Rose finishes Maggie's ponytail, then herds the two children into the bathroom to brush their teeth. She glances in the mirror and notices her first grey hair, leans in closer and spies a dozen or more. Rose pushes her hair aside and heads downstairs to make toast for Maggie and Liam. Her father is asleep at the dining-room table.

Lack

1997

Luke is gone three years, and Rose is still not very good at life. She stays up all night. Sometimes there are no clean clothes. The carrots in the crisper drawer are limp, and the apples are pocked with rot. On school days, Maggie and Liam wake early every morning, but they play quietly together because they know that if their mother doesn't wake until eight or later, she won't make them go to school. They are just settling back in after summer and already missing days.

On Saturday morning, Rose spends hours watching news clips of a princess's funeral on TV, with two and a half billion other people around the world. Nothing can protect you from this. Doesn't matter who you are.

There's nothing to eat.

Warm something until I'm done here, honey.

Cela bought Maggie a microwave oven for her tenth birthday, so that she could heat things without having to use the stove.

Warm some for Liam too, please.

I don't want anything.

Rose glances away from the TV toward Liam.

If you don't eat you'll die.

The coffin passes St. James's Palace, the princess's brother, her ex-husband, and her sons joining to walk behind. Black suits, white shirts, black ties. Her ex-husband's suit looks navy blue. On top of the coffin are three wreaths of white flowers from her brother and the boys. Tucked underneath one of the wreaths is a card addressed to *Mummy*. Rose tuts as she mutters to herself, a lump in her throat.

That's something. Them poor youngsters. Having to trail behind their mother like that. They're only babies. No one to look after them now, sure.

The coffin stops at the door of Westminster Abbey, its thousand-year-old towers rising two hundred and twenty-five feet into the sky. Inside, the coffin comes to rest. At the high altar, the great pavement is inlaid with stone of different colours, sizes, and shapes, made of onyx, purple porphyry, green serpentine, and yellow limestone, with pieces of opaque glass—red, turquoise, cobalt blue, and bluish white—mixed in. Her brother gives the eulogy.

"It is a point to remember that of all the ironies about my sister, perhaps the greatest was this—a girl given the name of the ancient goddess of hunting was, in the end, the most hunted person of the modern age."

Rose calls out to Maggie, who comes back into the family room, licking her finger.

Did you get anything?

I made an angel food cake in a mug. There's nothing else there.

I'll order some Mary Brown's or something. Give Emmy a bite too. This is nearly over.

Aside from milk, Mary Brown's is the only thing keeping Liam alive. He refuses to eat. When it gets too bad, Rose will pile everyone into the car and go get chicken strips and fries. Then she drives to the hospital and parks outside, threatening that if he doesn't eat, he'll have to go in. Liam will not be cowed by his mother. Maggie is afraid he's going into the hospital to die. She sits in the back seat, her hands clasped in her lap, praying that Liam will eat, Emily pulling at her hands from the car seat.

Rose clicks off the TV and stands up.

Come on guys, get your duds on. We're going for food.

Safe

Rose's mailing address is printed in large block letters, made
with a black marker on unlined white paper, which has been
plastered to opposite sides of an empty Dirt Devil box, with
reams of clear tape. Rose stows the box in the trunk of her
car, where it sits for years. She retrieves it from time to time
and rummages through, or adds to it, before resealing it and
returning it to the trunk. Rose used to think her mother went
overboard when doing up parcels to send across the country.
Now Rose understands the security that comes with swaddling
the contents, to protect them against the rigours of Canada
Post.

****

Cela fusses with her sister.

Rose, honey, you need to stop this. You need to stop thinking he was god.

Rose knows that she makes no sense to anyone. She doesn't
need to be told he was only a man. It's clear every time she lies
in her empty bed. And she understands that people don't get
it. She herself thought Trish was mad, or plain stupid, to think
that Gerald was going to swim fifty miles in out of it when the
boat went down. But Rose also thought that they must surely

have been run over by a foreign trawler and hauled aboard, that Luke was even now learning Russian, to get by until he could get away.

How does she tell someone that the first time she kissed Luke she imagined the home they would live in. How his kisses made her think about the purple patchwork quilt she made for him, with thick batting and the new plush backing you could buy. How when she told him that, he was hurt, wanting, she supposed, to stir something different in her. How his body crushing into hers made her believe in god. How the smell of orange chocolate makes her sick with missing him. How buying a new winter coat that she loves — navy and beige Aztec — makes her feel like she's cheating on him. How she doesn't have a picture of him with the baby because she was always waiting for him to get cleaned up or have a shave.

Rose can't shake the urge, every day, to crawl under something and lie down. Go deep into the woods to lick her wounds. She hates having to tell herself that he is not coming back in through that door. No matter how long she waits.

Rose thinks about the smell of Luke fading from the bedsheets that she has tucked away in the top drawer of his highboy. A year after he walked out the door for the last time, Rose packed the contents of the drawers into brown cardboard boxes to give away. Luke had not even taken the tags off one of the new pairs of jeans, and they meant nothing to her. She couldn't even imagine his smell on them. The bedsheets, and the denim shirt, and the emerald green silk, she kept for herself. The jean shirt had been waiting to be washed, but never was. Sometimes, when she got Maggie and Liam off to school, and Cela had done her visit on her way to work, Rose made a little mound in the centre of the bed with the sheets and the shirts, and lay the baby on it, then lay down and curled herself around Emily, burying her nose in the pile.

Now Emmy is four years old, and she has her own box of valuables, where she keeps her most important belongings. She knows that if their house burns down, or something else requires that they leave in a rush, she will not be allowed to stop and collect her things. She has to be ready to go. Emily does not know what the something else might be, but she is ready. Each night, she takes her teddy from the box, and nestles him into her bed. Teddy is a Beanie Baby, his weighted bottom allowing him to sit upright. He gazes at Emily from the pillow as she sleeps. Emily calls Teddy *she*, despite the red tie around his neck, very much a boy bear. Each morning, Emily opens the box and slips Teddy back inside, among her bracelets and hair combs and half-eaten lollipops, before sealing the cover tight on the green box with pink cabbage roses, and going about her four-year-old day.

**** **** *****

Rose writes a smaller note, neatly, on the front of a pink envelope, and signs it carefully. Before she tapes it securely to the end of the vacuum-cleaner box, Rose slips two twenty dollar bills inside the envelope, licks the flap, and seals it tight. The note and the money are insurance—if the car is ever stolen, Rose is depending on the thief's good nature to do what's right.

> *To Whom It May Concern,*
>> *This box contains my special things, photos of my family, and pictures and cards my children made.*
>> *I keep it here to protect it.*
>> *I truly do not care about the car.*
>> *But PLEASE send this box back to me. There is money inside for postage.*
>
>> *Sincerely,*
>> *Rose Tremblett*

Lucky

The bus does not stop for its last passengers here on its first pass through the tiny hamlet that is really an outskirt of town. It ambles along the narrow road, creaking as it twists and turns, rattling on the pocked pavement, until it reaches the edge of the hamlet itself, a stretch of road bordered on one side by an inlet, which continues many miles inland past the steel lift bridge spanning its mouth. Through the bus's left windows, the driver glances up a sheer incline, surveying the boulders balanced precariously along its face that defy the Department of Works Services and Transportation sign, warning vehicles of falling rocks. Rose stands at the bottom of the stairway and calls up.

Emily. Liam. You've got five minutes. The bus just passed.

Halfway along the stretch of road there is an outcrop of land with a single two-storey fishing stage, still owned by Pat Coates's family, where Luke and Barry used to mend nets. Rose would park her car at Luke's parents' house and walk to the stage for a visit.

The bus driver presses his boot on the brake and edges off the road before he swings the steering wheel with all his might, throwing the hulk of noisy yellow metal into a clumsy U-turn alongside the stage, then eases it back onto the road the way it came. Somewhere in the recesses of his brain, the driver is thankful for this makeshift turnaround.

Emily walks slowly down the lane and a few feet along the road to wait. She was upset when Maggie went to high school in September because Maggie always sat with her on the bus. She's glad Liam still takes her bus, even though he doesn't sit with her because he's in grade eight this year. He stands beside his friend Peter as they wait outside the bus-stop shelter that Peter's father built for them.

Maggie is relieved to be rid of the responsibility — she already sings Emily to sleep every night and takes her in the shower with her. When she was nine, Maggie changed Emily's diapers. And her mother won't stop dressing them alike. Maggie needs to distinguish herself in this family. Starting high school, she needs to distance herself, see if she can float on her own, live outside her mother's periphery. Dress like herself.

When Maggie was six, Rose still ordered matching outfits for her and Liam out of the catalogue, McKids colour-blocked outfits and black houndstooth bottoms with red sweatshirts, and teal and white polka-dotted shirts. When Rose took them to Disney when Maggie was nine, the summer after Luke was lost, she bought safari outfits, printed with lions hiding in leafy trees, green and yellow parrots with their heads cocked to one side. Maggie and Emily had one-piece short sets and Liam had khaki shorts with the patterned shirt, a grey plastic canteen hooked to his belt.

Rose wore a silky, khaki-coloured pantsuit, flying to Florida with her matching children, like a widow who is doing a good job. They each had a fake straw hat with a black brim; Maggie stuffed hers into her backpack. This year, after shopping with Maggie, her mother "coincidentally" bought Emily a baby-pink sweater and grey pants for the first day of school too. Rose waits for Maggie to get dressed every morning, then dresses Emily to match. Rose does not want to let Maggie go. A family that dresses together, stays together.

They hear the bus before it comes around the last turn and whines to a halt like some great leviathan heaving a sigh as its door flicks open long enough to allow the three children to shuffle up the steps, before it swallows them and lurches away. "Morning, Mr. English," Liam mutters as he reaches the top step. *Morning, Mr. English*, Emily thinks to herself. She doesn't look into his weathered old eyes, and she wonders why he has the word *cat*, in capital letters, across the front of his worn baseball cap. Mr. English was a heavy-equipment operator before he retired to driving school buses. Liam and Peter jostle down the empty aisle to the seats at the back of the bus. Emily sits alone a couple seats ahead. But Liam walks Emily to her classroom every morning and waits until the teacher arrives, often sprinting up the stairs to his own classroom as the last bell shrieks through the echoing hallways.

The bus stops once more in the hamlet before it staggers up Devil's Bit, Mr. English's boot nervously massaging the brake pedal as the bus heaves down the other side of the steep hill. Emily counts each stop along the way, until she reaches four, and her belly flutters. She stares out the window at the man and the girl waiting. She knows who they are, knows he fished with her father. Knows he had the flu. The man's name is Barry and the girl's name is Kayla. He has a full beard and a huge gut and he always wears big rubber boots. Barry stands on the side of the road with his hands lazing in the pockets of his navy work pants, which are stuffed into his green logans. He went back to fishing a few years ago because he had no choice. His hand rises from his pocket in a small wave as Kayla motions at him through the closing door. Emily's fingers graze the condensation on the windowpane.

Barry watches the bus as it eases into a lineup of cars waiting for the lift bridge to lower so they can be on their way again. Kayla is in grade four, and she is a girl who looks like she doesn't give a fuck. She has straight, dirty-blond hair that creeps down each shoulder from a centre part, without any trappings of buckles or bows. Blue eyes full of devilment in a chubby face with a high forehead, her two front teeth looking very adult surrounded by the baby teeth that are still hanging on. She wears grey sweatpants, white socks, and sneakers with a hint of pink in the Nike flash across their side. As she takes her seat, her fall jacket swings open over a grimacing Hulk Hogan face on a yellow T-shirt. There is nothing special about her appearance, but Emily's belly flutters every time she sees Kayla and her dad. Emily stares at Kayla's face as she approaches, clear skin and red cheeks. Not a freckle to be seen. She doesn't know how lucky she is.

Kayla's is the last stop before school. The kids who live on the other side of the bridge are walkers. As the bus eases into the lineup of vehicles and stops there, Emily feels the same way her mother did years ago, like she is on display, her fingers worrying themselves in her lap and her toes curling themselves inside her brown suede boots. Her eyes are fixed on the head of blond hair now sitting three rows ahead of her.

Sever

2001

The first string Rose cuts is the salon. On a Wednesday in July, Rose concludes that it's time to go to school if she's ever going. On Friday, she decides to sell the salon and all its contents to the girls she works with every day. No soft place to land in case she falls. At the end of August, Rose takes a black cape, two grey combs, and the oblong case that holds her scissors, dragons and fans spread across the red cover, and locks the salon door for the last time. She is moving to town. But Rose keeps Luke's house.

Emily is going into grade two, in a new school, new surroundings, in the city. Rose is registered for an introduction to psychology and an English course at the university and has rented an old house in St John's. She promises Maggie and Liam that they can come home again for grades eleven and ten next year, if they're not happy. Rose gets a job tending bar four nights a week (the tips are good), drops the kids at three separate schools, and sleeps from late morning until two.

****

Just as Rose is rushing in the door from school, the cable guy shows up for her appointment. It is an unusually hot September day, and the overweight man is already sweating as he climbs the stairs to Rose's bedroom, where the TV sits in an old pine armoire. The humid air is stifling in the old house, whose open windows do little, the sheer panels that are pushed aside barely stir. The man swelters through the installation, grumbling. Rose perches on the double bed behind him, feet dangling over the side of the high wrought-iron frame, wishing he would finish. He pulls on his belt buckle and swipes at his forehead with his sleeve. Rose feels bad for the man, but she wants him out of the way so she can get back to the breaking news alerts that are screaming from every radio and TV in North America. Every television around the world.

Rose was sitting in psychology class with three hundred other students when the professor announced that the World Trade Center had been hit by an airplane. Stunned silence. Then people whispering to each other.

Is this a test?

This is some kind of psychological experiment.

I don't think he should be allowed to do this.

I am telling you, this is not a joke.

Rose is transfixed by the images flashing on her television screen, black clouds billowing from the tower. Frozen to her bed, Rose watches another plane burst into flame as it slices through the far side of the second tower, lower than the first strike. Rose has no idea how long she sits there, but she looks away when the anchor announces that the debris falling from the buildings is actually people.

****

Rose decides that she needs to get her shit together. She'll put Emmy in an after-school program, and Maggie and Liam can bus home, allowing her an extra hour or two to rest during the afternoons. She needs to be serious about this new life she has imagined. The first day that Emily will attend after-school care, Rose gets a call from Hazelwood Elementary at two forty-five. She turns over in the bed, reaches for her phone on the nightstand.

Mrs. Tremblett? You forgot to pick Emily up?

Rose bolts upright, wide awake.

The program attendant didn't pick her up?

There was no one here from a program to pick her up. She is still waiting for you.

Someone else was supposed to pick her up. I'm sorry. I'm sorry, tell her I'm coming.

Rose backs out of the driveway without looking both ways and honks her horn at the car crawling up Topsail Road in front of her.

Mommy is coming, Mommy is coming, she says loudly to the car.

When Emily sees her mother push through the glass door, her tears fall.

I'm sorry Emmy, Mommy is sorry. You won't have to go to the after-school program again.

When they get home, Rose calls the program administrator to demand an explanation.

She wasn't on our list for pickup today. Are you sure you had it arranged?

I had it arranged. I was in there only three days ago, and the owner herself squeezed Emmy in for me. My daughter spent an hour there, and I came and got her.

A long hour, Rose wants to say. Emily was not happy to stay there without her mother, not happy with people she didn't know.

Well, we didn't have her on the list. Of course, you won't be charged for your first visit, or for today.

Rose spits her fright and anger into the phone.

I won't be charged? I? Won't be charged? You'll be very lucky if I don't have you charged. I wouldn't bring my child back there if you paid me. Not one penny will you ever see from me. And I'll be telling people too.

Rose slams the receiver into its cradle. How dare they risk her child like that. Fuck sakes. Proves if you want anything done right. . .

Rose is early at Hazelwood every afternoon now, waits in the porch, to make sure that Emily sees her when she gets out. To prove that she's a good mother. At the end of the school year, Rose packs up the mess and goes back to Luke's house. Liam has already moved back out to live with Rose's mother and father, exhausting Rose in his refusal to go to school. Maggie can get back to her boyfriend and her committees, and Emily can land safely in Nanny Tremblett's arms, who will walk her down to the shop again for a Charleston Chew bar, and run it under warm water for Emily until the chocolate coating melts away, to the white nougat inside that she likes. Rose will spend the next two years driving the highway to St. John's, loving school enough to ignore the dark circles under her eyes.

Pat Byrne is her favourite professor. From Great Paradise, the same little outport as her father. Pat tells her not to listen to the student advisers, to do English for herself and worry about a job with her next degree. Rose likes people who think the way she does. She laughs through his classes, watching him get a rise out of the eighteen-year-olds.

The Oxford comma is, as my poor old father would say, like dry shit on a blanket. Neither harm nor good.

He doesn't blink as the teenagers stare at him. Stunned.

Sixteen

Rose gets Liam a dog for his sixteenth birthday—he's had a rough couple years, spent the last half of last year living with Rose's parents. Couldn't stand another day in St. John's, so Rose let him go home with them to finish the school year.

Now, even though they're all home in Ferndale again, Liam just can't force himself to stay at school. Rose drives him there every morning on her way to St. John's, and he leaves early every day. Sometimes he sits on the rocky beach across the street from the school, trying to convince himself to go back inside for the afternoon. At least then he'd be able to take the bus. But Liam always leaves and walks for miles every day to get home. When Mr. Pitts makes a comment in the hallway one morning to embarrass Liam, Rose goes to the school. The principal says Liam will get an apology from Mr. Pitts, and Rose tells him an apology only means something if it doesn't happen again.

The dog is an attempted apology for the world being shitty. Something nice that Liam can call his own. Rose names the dog before she brings him home though. She doesn't want another Daisy the Terminator—which is what you get when two kids are old enough to name a toy poodle. When Rose arrives at the pet store in Carbonear to pick up the dog, she questions whether he is only eight weeks old, legs long and lean like a thoroughbred. He and his brother are looking for homes and it's all she can do not to take both. They are Heinz 57s, one white with brown patches like a beagle, the other, black and white—he's friendlier, not as shy. Rose chooses the dog with the brown patches, his intelligent eyes telling her he's the one. Harley.

Rose uses her children's first and middle names when she's angry at them or giving stern orders. When she is upset with the dog, she yells, "Harley Yafucker." So Liam christens him Harley Yafucker Tremblett. Rose sits at the desktop typing with two fingers, swearing at her school assignments, and Liam says the dog thinks she's mad at him.

Eight weeks or not, Harley is no more than a puppy for sure. He flies around the house pouncing, chewing up everything he gets his paws on. He eats one of Maggie's pink stilettos she bought out of her first cheque from waitressing at the hotel on weekends. Maggie sits Harley down and tells him she is very upset.

Seventy dollars. Do you know what it takes to earn seventy dollars? A whole Saturday. I know you're only a baby, but you have to learn better than that, Harley.

Maggie tucks the second shoe away in her closet because she can't bear the thought of throwing it away.

When Harley races into the living room, Rose and Maggie grab cushions for cover, knowing that Harley will take a single leap and land squarely on top of one of their heads before bouncing away again.

Liam wants the best food for Harley, though he still doesn't eat enough himself to keep a bird alive. He has a low tolerance for variety in foods. When Rose finds something that Liam likes—which is only ever some version of chicken strips or pizza—he eats it every day, sometimes for a year, until he turns himself from it. Then Rose spends weeks or months finding a replacement. Sometimes Liam is still tolerating a food and the manufacturer decides to make a new and improved version. Liam has not once found it to be an improvement.

Liam also doesn't take well to other teenagers, especially ones he doesn't know. Sounds are amplified for Liam. Rose walks into his bedroom and he is watching a TV show, the characters having a heated argument, but the volume is so low Rose can't hear it. Liam has the hearing of a dog. The noise from a crowd of teens is like gongs, beaten over and over. The sound seeps into his skin.

Once, on a Saturday evening, Peter and his friends coaxed Liam to go to the track with them. Rose spent more than one night hanging out on the track herself, but these are good boys who she's known since they were five, and she encourages him to go. "It'll be nice, Liam. Just be careful." She slips some money into his pocket.

There are more people than Liam expects, and he stands on the edge of the crowd, sipping a Molson Canadian, watching. Embers from the fire crackle and fly into the air as more wood is thrown on, tree branches and wood chunks and pieces of broken board.

Suddenly, someone yells, Run, and the crowd disappears into the trees.

Rose answers a knock on the door and Liam is standing there, flanked by two men in dark bomber jackets and jeans.

Hello Mrs. Tremblett. I'm Officer Lannon, and this is Officer Boucher. Is this your son?

It is.

His name?

Liam.

He's not in big trouble or anything. We just broke up a little party that your son says he doesn't know much about, so we thought we'd bring him home to you. So you know.

You scared me. I thought something was wrong.

They say a few more words then give their goodbyes. Rose touches Liam's arm as the Mounties walk away.

They said they were cops, Mom, but they didn't show any badges. I didn't have a clue. It could've been anybody locking me in the back of their car.

When Liam finally gets a girlfriend, Rose is happy for him, but she dreads the hurt he'll inevitably face. She wishes she could protect him. She drops him off at the girlfriend's house one evening, and he's back an hour later. Liam doesn't answer his mother's questions. Months later, Rose finds out that the girl told Liam she loved him, and he broke up with her and walked all the way home.

Liam loves Harley. The dog lives in his bedroom and follows him around. Liam house-trains Harley, shows him the ins and outs of giving his paw and high fives. And teaches him to stay.

Little Pond

Maggie is crying uncontrollably when Rose gets home, her pink pillow sham stained dark with tears and snot.

Oh my. What's going on?

They won't let me walk with Mollie.

Who won't let you walk with Mollie?

In the Grand March. They won't let us.

And why won't they let ye, now?

Oh Mom, I don't know. The art teacher, Ani, said it was fine and she's in charge of the Grand March, but Mr. Pitts said absolutely not.

So Mr. Pitts is the boss, is he?

Rose rolls her eyes and heaves a sigh, exhaling deeply. She knows this one is not going to be resolved in a day.

Rose spends the next week campaigning with the girls, who have met with the prom committee and gathered signatures on a petition. The principal asks them to put their concerns in writing, which Rose helps them to do. After several more meetings and conversations, Mr. Hickman tells Rose this is not something he can make a decision on and would she be willing to talk in front of the school council if he invited her to their Thursday meeting.

I'll speak in front of whoever I have to, Leonard.

All right then, I'll get it arranged.

When Rose arrives on Thursday evening, the group is already assembled, and they all know the details of Rose's grievance because everyone has been talking about it for days. That's fine with Rose, she doesn't mind playing their game. She slips the letter out of her bag and reads it to the assembled judges. Rose talks about how Maggie has always been an active member of the school community, stepping forward to volunteer for whatever needed to be done. Rose names a few of the extracurricular and other activities that her daughter participates in: she is on the student council; sits on the recycling, library, and just about every other committee there is; helps with the school lunch program; volunteers at the hospital; is passionate about the rights of students and equity for all. She knows the difference between treating people equally and treating them equitably—everyone has different needs and different starting points. Rose goes on and on.

When she's finished, they sit staring at her as if she's just served them a bowl of gruel. All of them toeing the line. Rose is relieved she wore dress pants and a blazer this evening, the group sitting in judgment in their cardigans and pearls. She attempts to cut through the condescension.

What do you think, May?

These are people who have watched her daughter grow up. Watched Rose raise her children alone. May brought a casserole to the house after Luke's service.

Well, I can't really go against the decision that's been made.

Oh. Well then. I guess I'm wasting my time. I thought I was invited here to have a discussion that would lead to consideration of what's being said. I thought I knew most of you well enough to believe that you'd listen to reason. My mistake.

Rose's voice trembles. It drives her crazy that tears are so close when she's fighting for what she knows is right.

We're talking about letting a couple girls walk together in the Grand March. It's not rocket science, guys.

Mr. Hickman intervenes.

There's no need for anyone to get upset here, now. There are other considerations to be taken into account. For example, there's some concern that this could make some of the other students feel uncomfortable or left out. What about the girls... or boys... who haven't been asked to walk?

What about them indeed, Mr. Hickman. This would do the exact opposite of what you appear to think it would. This would allow kids who haven't been asked to walk to feel more comfortable, not less. Maybe other girls would like to walk in pairs.

Well, that's part of it too, actually. If too many girls decide to walk together, there won't be enough partners for the boys.

Are you serious? You're serious. You expect an exodus of the whole female student population, do you? Because of two girls, who've been best friends since they were born, and who decided when they were twelve that they'd walk together for prom. You all know these kids. They're not trying to cause a riot. It didn't even occur to them that this would be an issue.

Our decision remains unchanged.

Well, I'll just say one more thing before I go, Leonard. I hope you all realize how very lucky you are that this is Maggie and Mollie. Because you could find yourself in serious hot water, I think, if this request was being made by a young same-sex couple. I'd suggest that you take that into consideration if you're ever faced with this situation again. Because you very likely will be. We can't live in the dark ages forever.

Rose drives home with the radio off. She can't believe this, just can't believe it. Like the goddamn Harper Valley PTA. Rose sits for a long time in the car before she goes in the house to tell Maggie.

Next morning, Maggie calls her mother from school at break time.

I came in this morning, Mom, and Mr. Pitts told me that we can walk together in the prom.

Gap

2004

When Maggie graduates, she decides to go to Université Sainte-Anne in Pointe-de-l'Église, Nova Scotia, because she is accepted into the immersion program and will be sorry if she doesn't go. She's been wanting to stay home. But she's a grown-up now, and she can't change her life plans to be a French teacher just because she's not ready to leave. Maggie teases her mother that it won't be cooked meals she'll miss — every takeout french fry she eats will make her long for home.

Rose wants to be back in the city. Cela has already moved there. Liam and Emily will manage. And this time, Luke's brothers have bought the house that Luke built, for their mother. So Rose can't return.

Rose is excited for Maggie. She books two tickets to fly to Halifax and rents a car to drive the three hours from there. She'll see for herself where Maggie will be settling in. Maggie spends her last night in Newfoundland in St. John's with her friends, and Rose stays behind to pack the last of her daughter's things into boxes to ship. She'll pick Maggie up on the way to the airport. Rose gathers jeans, shoes, boots, purses, and belts. She slips each of Maggie's sweaters off their hangers and folds them into a long, low box on the floor.

The last sweater is one Rose bought her at Gap the Christmas she was in grade eight. A bulky slouch knit, stripes of red and lime green and royal blue running in circles, interspersed with rings of heavy ivory wool. Still Maggie's favourite. She wears it often because it's warm, its big turtleneck swallowing Rose's little girl. Rose spreads the sweater atop the box, folds the body in thirds lengthwise, tucks the sleeves, and arranges the neck to lie neatly at the centre. She places the colourful sweater on top of the others and stares at Maggie's belongings. Now what is she supposed to do? She kneels down and runs her hands over the contents, leans into the box, hugging it tight as she buries her face, the sounds that escape her muffled by the sweater.

As winter blows across the island from Nova Scotia, Rose finds a house in the city. Not a sensible house. Not a suitable house for a woman on her own. Cela's eyebrows arch when Rose tells her she looked at a two-hundred-year-old house. The oldest house in St. John's.

Leave it to you.

Cela, I really just need you to talk me out of it. Come see it with me. Tell me what you think.

I can already tell you what I think.

Just come with me. Say hello.

Say hello to a house.

You know what I mean, Cela. Just come. It has such personality.

Rose calls the owner again. He gives her the combination to the lockbox and Rose and Cela shovel their way in to the house with green and red trim. The crust of snow scatters, broken by the metal tip of the shovel.

Cela has to admit there's a certain appeal, peaked roof with gingerbread trim, skinny icicles dangling from its front eaves like a crystal garland strung on a Christmas tree. Cela peeks in the porch window over Rose's shoulder while Rose jiggles the key, age spots on the pine floor marring its shellac, a path worn to bare board along the middle of the narrow hallway.

The rooms are bigger than Cela thought they seemed through the window. There's a fireplace in the dining room and a spacious living room through the doorway across the hall. There are three fireplaces in all, two in bedrooms on the second floor, either of which would make a respectable master. Cela decides the one farthest from the bathroom is the winner—its ceiling is better and the original double doors to the shallow closet add an air of authority, a silver tassel hanging from a marble doorknob. The fireplace has a die-cut metal surround that follows the curve of the hearth, a matte-black tool set nestled in the corner.

Cela follows Rose up the second flight of stairs. The higher they go the dizzier she gets. Rose could do things with this place. The third floor has sloped ceilings and a dormer window looking out onto the backyard.

That whole space wouldn't belong to you, would it?

Yep. Used to be three separate gardens that the owner bought, and he's willing to sell it all with the house.

That's quite a parcel of land.

So are you not talking me out of it?

Cela hunches her shoulders.

You have to get it I guess, Rose. It just screams you, doesn't it.

Reminder

2005

Rose has a memory box that she bought at the mall when Maggie was little. Maggie hated when her mother got sucked into Bombay Company every time they tried to pass by. So many breakable things that she wasn't allowed to touch. Barely enough space to walk, between rows of coloured glass vases on glass shelves, gold cushions with fringes and tassels, so many piled in the armchairs that Maggie was afraid they'd fall out if she brushed against them as she squeezed by, and dark wooden four-poster beds festooned with even more cushions, fat and fringed and sequined. Maggie was forced to trail behind her mother, who wouldn't let her sit on a bench just outside the door, even though it was within eyesight, or look into the mirrors with flower garlands across their tops, or get too close to the sparkly picture frames that stood in a long line on a skinny black table. Maggie was relieved when her Mom asked her if she liked the shiny brown box that looked like a book, with a hiding place under the cover. It meant they'd head to the checkout and then finish their real Christmas shopping.

A small brass plaque to attach to the box's cover was included, and Rose got it engraved at a little shop before leaving the mall.

Luke Tremblett
April 25, 1961 - October 13, 1994

The engraver used a hyphen instead of a dash to separate the dates. It's the one thing that still bothers Rose.

Years after she bought it, Rose still goes to the mahogany box when she can't sleep, or when she's cooped up in the house for too many days. Nine years after she bought it, there are still nights when Rose can't sleep and still days when she can't leave the house. No matter what she finds to fill her life with, sometimes the box is the only place she finds comfort. The fleur-de-lys brass hinges have turned green and the plaque is dappled with corrosion—the hyphen has disappeared and the tiny screws have haloes of tarnish. Rose opens the cover and fingers the poem she wrote, sitting on top of the pile.

First Son
I wonder
Which brother'll cut enough wood
To keep the stovetop red this winter
Now who'll tackle
Trying to please the ol' man
D'ol man
That's the only thing I ever heard him called
D'ol man
He'd grunt
The old man stands on his sagging front step
Wind and rain lashing
Slack suspenders on his back
Gnarled hands and face
Upturned to deaf black sky
There's a faded photo somewhere in a box
The old man young

Standing on that front step
Smiling
His first baby son in his arms

Underneath are pictures of Maggie and Liam and Emily. Rose still tucks things away in there every now and then. A small journal that Maggie gave her. Maggie brings journals to her mother as gifts. Rose tries to use them, but she doesn't want to spoil them with her jot notes. The parchment sheets of the journal in the box are pristine.

There are pages torn from tiny spiral notebooks with birthday messages to Luke, and scraps of paper with love notes scribbled down. *I was home at 430 to 530 gone to do a net Will be home at around 8 Love you Luke Hope you had a good day Love Luke.* Snaps of the house before it was finished, the wood still a bright blond, wishes printed on paper four-leaf clovers by Maggie and Liam, a Fishing Master IV Certificate in a navy-blue hardback cover, newspaper clippings from the accident and two identical birthday cards, bought three years apart. The cards were pure proof, according to Luke, that he meant every word, having paid for them twice.

There is the beginning of a letter that Rose is writing to Nate. Pages of loose leaf, brightly coloured construction and graph paper. As Emily grew she added her own sheets to the box, raising the lid, slipping her pictures and notes inside. A pencil drawing of a mommy, a daddy, and a little girl, straight lines of hair traced over and over. Her first printing on a page with broken lines. *A A A.*

Everyone sending messages through space and time. *Are you in Love with me Love Luke.*

Clock

Muscle sinew bone, muscle sinew bone — Rose steps through the wall and Luke is not there waiting. She heads through to the dining room, where he is slouched in the armchair by the window, his lips moving as she walks toward him.

I have something for you.

Well give it here.

Rose bends and places her lips at his right eyebrow, straightens as if bowing, bends and kisses his left. Luke puts his arms around her waist and she leans her forehead to his.

You have to go get it yourself.

His mouth arching.

It's in the closet, Rosie.

Rose moves the length of the galley kitchen and feels Luke's gaze follow her. She opens the folding door.

I don't see anything. There's nothing here.

Look harder.

Rose glances at each end of the closet and finally sees a large flat box slid behind the hot water boiler. She pokes her head inside the door and reaches in for the box. She is glad the door shields her face as she catches a glimpse of the picture on the front. It is a plastic wall clock. A brown, plastic, faux-wood clock.

Happy birthday, hun.

Luke joins her in the kitchen and kisses her on the lips while she pulls the clock from its package. The brown plastic has gold columns running the length of each side and a plastic swinging pendulum hanging between two circular cut-outs in its lower section. Three small clear plastic bags taped to its side contain more gold accents to attach at one's leisure. There are two half spheres which, on closer inspection, contain maps of each hemisphere that slide into slots above the columns, and a rearing horse for the top.

A grandfather clock. You've always wanted a grandfather clock.

Rose looks from the clock to Luke's face, so sincere looking back at her.

I love it. Thank you.

It matches the jewellery box I got you. Almost exactly.

It does. Exactly. Thank you, my darling.

Rose hugs him tightly as she pictures the tiny plastic ballerina twirling to the music every morning when she raises its lid. Rose has learned to appreciate absurdity.

And what's this, Luke?

Rose's gaze falls to the countertop.

Flour.

Flour.

It's flour. You've always promised to make me bread.

Luke's tone suggests that this is another gift Rose will be powerless to resist.

I have promised. And today is the day. You'll have bread for supper. Now, find batteries for the clock while I get started.

Luke takes the clock, the arch back in his lip, and busies himself with getting it hung while Rose reaches for the bag of flour and reads the directions on the back. Luke rummages through drawers and underneath the sink, assembles his necessary tools, and implores Rose's opinion and approval, as he tries one spot, then another, before settling on the perfect placement so that the clock can be viewed from all angles. By the time he stows his hammer and level away, Rose is sprinkling flour on the counter and kneading the dough, turning it in clockwise motions and pressing her fists into its centre as she remembers watching her mother do. Luke half whispers into her hair as he encircles her waist from behind.

Aren't we the two old fogies?

Yeah, the only thing missing is the underwear Mom used to wear on her head to keep her hairs out of the pan.

Rose allows herself to fold into his body. The afternoon passes with sporadic attention paid to the rising dough and the lowering sun, until the day is spent and the smell of fresh bread reaches up and drags them downstairs to the kitchen again.

Suppertime.

Luke stretches the word out as he glances at the clock. He pulls the bread from the oven, wincing at the hot crust as he stands the loaf on end with his bare hands and cuts thick slices to toast. Rose boils the kettle and prepares two mugs of sweet milky tea as Luke piles a tower of buttery toast on a plate for them to share.

Is there anything you can't do?

Luke bites into the soggy toast as if it is light as a cloud.

Not much we can't do, together.

When they've finished their toast and tea, Luke lays the plate on the table beside the armchair, settles back, and scoops Rose onto his lap. She wriggles until she's comfortable, nestles her head into the spot where his neck meets his shoulder, and listens to his heartbeat. She lies quietly until his head dips and his breathing becomes measured, and then she gets up to go.

Rose whispers, *Muscle sinew bone, muscle sinew bone*, and steps back through the living-room wall, into grey October.

Floored

1994

Rose climbs out of the car and stands at the low-slung gate of the house she grew up in. She extends her hand and the gate pushes open, places one foot in front of the other on the red brick walkway that leads to the step, reaches for the green wooden handrail, and walks in the front door. She fills her chest with air as she takes in the flowered wallpaper and a white closet rod that spans the width of the small porch, coats hanging on wire and plastic hangers. The rod is secured on opposite sides with two-by-fours nailed to the walls. There are shoes piled in a wooden box beneath the coat rack. Rose opens the door into the dining room, the same garlands of flowers running around its walls, and turns the corner to the living room without breaking stride.

When she sees her father's face, framed by the ugly khaki of the plaid couch, her knees give way, and she crawls the remaining distance to the centre of the living room, where she lies flat on her back on the beige linoleum, feet on the floor, knees jutting to the ceiling.

I don't know what he was thinking. I can't do this.

Her father pulls himself from his seat and kneels above Rose's head, cradles her temples in his hands, and kisses her forehead.

You are stronger than you think.

Rose clasps her father's hands, hooking her fingernails into his palms.

I don't want to be.

He squeezes her hands tightly, then lies beside her on the cold floor.

After staring at the ceiling until Rose's breathing calms, her father tells her the story of the only trip he made to the Arctic. It happened the year after he and Mom were married, when Abbey was four months old. He was the last in line, crossing the ice at dusk with three other men, heading back to the ship. They walked slowly in the cold, a fair distance between them, to distribute their weight on the ice, with fault lines criss-crossing it, like the cracked palms inside their gloves. He took a step and the ice gave way beneath him. Disappeared. The cold jolted his body like electricity. Encasing him. Water surged around his eyes and his ears and his nose. How his throat scalded with the thought of her mother getting the news. Ice above his head. No footing below. Breathing water. He does not tell her the story of his rescue.

He was thinking about you and the baby, Rosie. He was thinking about you.

Heart

As the oldest child, and because of her nature, Maggie has always been Rose's helper. Her glossy dark hair is long and she puts it in ponytails a lot. It is as fine now as when she was a baby. And her tears are as remarkable. Rose thought she'd grow into her tears, but they've grown bigger, brimming over long lashes unable to hold them, spilling down her cheeks. Maggie is bright and bubbly and beautiful. She loves dressing up and high heels. Rose tells people she is as nice as she is pretty. Her high school friends still call her when they need someone to talk to. Maggie has a therapeutic presence. She is the kind of person who will save the world, if she's not crushed by it. She says the kids who bullied her—who found her girliness irresistible and teased her every day—made her strong. She forbade her mother's involvement. She wishes she were taller. She wants to be a teacher. She is happy at university. She loves hard and she plays nice.

Emily uses the fact that she is the baby to her advantage, even though she's thirteen years old. She is Rose's only red-head—a true melded auburn in winter, her hair shattering into reds and browns in summer sunshine. She spends hours with flatirons, erasing all traces of her untamed curls. Her skin is so fair that tiny blue veins show just below the surface around her eyes, but she never gets sunburned. Emily knew all the words to "Don't Cry for Me Argentina," before she was three and belted it in her baby soprano every chance she got. She played piano but laid it aside and is learning to play guitar, even though no one who belongs to her has a note in their body. As a baby, she would toddle over and climb into her mother's lap for a back massage. She still crawls into Rose's bed and whispers as she falls asleep, "Rub my back." She's torn between the pride of honour roll and the embarrassment of nerd. There are early indications that she will give Rose a run for her money.

As the middle child, Liam struggles with finding his place. When they were little, only born a year apart, Liam and Maggie were best friends. When they came home from the playground, Maggie told Rose that Liam talked to everyone there, while she sat and waited for him. And he was brave, she said. Once Maggie ran all the way home and got Granddad to come with her to rescue Liam from the top of the jungle gym. Rose's seventy-two-year-old father had to scale the bars to reach him, balancing himself on his hands and knees while he persuaded Liam it was safe to climb down. As teenagers, Liam and Maggie reversed roles — Maggie was the social butterfly and Liam had to push himself to attend family functions but only sometimes did. He dresses in T-shirts and hoodies, always shades of grey or oatmeal, baggy jeans so long that his runners have scooped out ragged half-moons at his heels. He keeps his brown hair clippered with a three-quarter-inch guard over his entire head. He likes to leave the traces of sideburns and whiskers that have appeared on his face. He is brilliant and tolerant and full of anxiety. Rose's kisses have long since lost their healing power. Liam's height is checked by his rounded shoulders, his head bent slightly forward and down. He looks as if a touch would make him curl in like a caterpillar.

In ten years, Nate will be older than his father. He is already a father himself. When he visited as a younger teenager, Emily would hide by the end of the couch and ease her way out as she warmed up to him. Nate lived with Rose for four months to finish high school and work for the summer, after his mother moved to town. Nate and Rose did not remain as close as Rose intended, but when he comes home they see each other, and Nate's wife confides in Rose and keeps her updated from time to time. When she needed someone to talk to she said, "Rose, I'm glad I have you." The older Nate gets, the more like Luke he becomes, the same fire in his beard and in his heart. Nate had a baby before he was twenty, and he went through some rough patches over the years and made some really unhealthy choices that Rose attributed to his father dying, and Rose worried about him, worried that he missed so much by losing Luke. But Nate stuck it out and grew up and learned that family matters most. Rose wrote Nate a letter, telling him how proud his dad would be of him.

Muffins and Fries

2009

Emily wants to go to PWC. The better high school, she says—
not that she cares too much, but why should the fries be the
only ones allowed to transfer there? Rose is happy to oblige her
by telling the lie necessary to get her in, even though she's not
in French immersion. "Yes, my daughter lives with my sister
on Thorburn Road." The girl on the desk says, "Yes, I understand." She knows what's going on. "You'll just have to bring
in a piece of mail with your sister's name on it, and a note indicating the arrangement." Cela will roll her eyes over this. Rose
and Emily drive home together, satisfied.

Rose is relieved. Not that she believes that only the smart
kids are in the bilingual program. Or that one group is better
than the other. Or that it's the friends' fault when a child steps
out of line. But PWC *is* the better high school. Emily keeps
her two groups of friends completely separate—her french
fries, as she calls the immersion girls, and her English muffins, who are not in the immersion program so do not attend
PWC because they're zoned for Holy Heart, and not all mothers are willing to bend the rules to get their daughters what
they want. It doesn't hurt that this means Emily will spend
her days with the fries, who happen to be a more conservative
lot of girls.

But Emily continues to straddle the fence, hopping back and forth between the muffins and the fries. And starting grade ten at PWC doesn't make her anxiety go away. She still misses way too much school, and spends too much time in the guidance counsellor's office when she's there. The counsellor is advising her about which subjects are best for her to do each semester. Rose doesn't agree with his decisions, but Emily is happy to take the easy options, giving little thought to what she'll do when she graduates. High school was easier in the bay, without the choices, all students studying the same core subjects, and the only big decision was whether to do honours or academic math.

Emily keeps a journal because writing stuff on paper helps to calm the jumble in her head. But she leaves some of it clanking around in there because she worries that her mother might read it. Emily asks Maggie what she did to keep her private things private. What happened if Mom learned her secrets?

Mom will never read your diary. Never, Emmy.

How can you be so sure?

Because I know. I didn't used to trust her either, but I tested her. And she was serious when she said all she wanted was honesty and she'd never invade my privacy. She said she just had to take my word for it because what's the use of anything if you don't have trust.

Yeah, she says the same thing to me.

She means it. Mom is lots of things, Emmy, she drives me nuts too, but you can take her word for it. She won't touch your diary.

Emily shares different information with her muffins and her fries, but if she ever really needs advice she usually goes to Maggie. And she tells the guidance counsellor what he wants to hear. Her mother is content as long as she knows where Emily is most of the time, and that she is managing at school.

Emily is smart like Rose was—never cracks a book, crams everything in at the last minute, and she's restless with the constraints of teenagehood. Too much like her mother for her own good. And Rose's.

Profile

2010

hey_by
Smart. Funny. Just left of normal.
Looking for same.

I like:
Old houses
Dictionaries
Baileys
Laughing till I cry
Pubs
Sunshine
Sisters
Neat beards
Smiles
Scrabble
Straight shooters
Stand-up comedy
Hammocks
High heels
Holding hands
Bear hugs

I dislike:
Intolerance
Cold
Standing in lineups
Parking meters
Screech-ins

Walking alone in the dark
Parallel parking
One-word introductions
LOL-ing when nothing funny was said

Not much beats good company and great conversation. And
sometimes a cold beer and laughter is all that's needed to make
an evening.
Hope everyone finds what they're looking for!

Cela says that online dating is the way to go. Rose is uncertain as to how Cela acquired this knowledge, given that she's married to Don, whom she started dating when she was thirteen years old. Rose is not sure she can trust Cela's judgment on things she only knows from hearsay, after the Brazilian fiasco, when she had assured Rose that "an aesthetician is a pro, you'll hardly know she's at it." Rose had only ever shaved before. She winced as she eased back in behind the steering wheel and called Cela before she left the parking lot. "Jesus Cela, do you secretly hate me or what? Sending me to get that done on my lunch break?" Cela had laughed. "I'm sorry, Rosie, but you're a bit of a drama queen. You'll be glad you did it when the sting goes out of it. You'll thank me."

Cela offers something about a friend of a friend who met the love of her life online. Everyone seems to be doing it. Cela and Don cajole Rose into putting up her own profile, and Rose returns the favour by regaling them with online stories whenever she gets a chance. Rose is not entirely comfortable with having her picture online but Cela says she has to put herself out there and the site says she will get ten times more responses with a picture. And even more than that if she smiles. Cela says don't be judgmental and be nice to people, so Rose tries to answer all the messages.

your conversation with heyletschat5555
heyletschat5555
What turns you on creatively, spiritually, or emotionally?

> hey_by
> hmmmm… had no idea there was gonna be a test
> 1) I'm an interior decorator (of sorts) and get my creative
> release there
> 2) belief in something
> 3) intelligent conversation

heyletschat5555

> hey_by
> :)

That's as skilled as Rose gets in the emoticon department, and she moves on to another message, her attention already waning.

your conversation with ready_to_go_again
ready_to_go_again
Hi gorgeous
I had to stop in and tell you that
Wow
I am hoping to be moving to town in a week or two
Maybe we'll run into each other
:)) Lol

> hey_by
> ya never know who ya might run into : -)

Rose shakes her head. She will have to keep her eyes peeled for ready to go again.

your conversation with keeptruckin
keeptruckin
hi

hey_by
hi :)

keeptruckin
how are you

hey_by
i'm good. How are you?

keeptruckin
im good too

Rose thinks it's great that keeptruckin' got *too* right. But she doesn't think she has the chutzpah to develop these types of messages into conversations. When they get marginally better, she agrees to go bowling with a guy. Rose bowled once when she was a teenager. She arrives at Plaza Bowl five minutes early because she believes in punctuality. As the door swings closed behind her, she sizes up the back of a man who is perusing the bulletin board at the top of the stairs. His faded brown hair skims a denim collar above narrow shoulders that taper to narrower hips. His shirt is tucked into jeans held up by a black leather belt pocked with shiny silver studs. The jeans are tucked into red genuine crocodile-skin cowboy boots.

Jim?

He turns slowly, revealing a long goatee and thin cheeks topped off by mirrored eyeglasses. Sometimes a camera adds more than ten pounds.

Rose?

Yes.

How did you know it was me, Rose?

I just had a feeling.

They shake hands, then descend the steps into the bowling alley, where they rent multicoloured lace-up shoes that look better than the crocodile boots. In the coming days, Rose figures a way to refuse further bowling dates while appearing fair-minded and nonjudgmental. Rose is not convinced she is cut out for this.

> your conversation with justlookin320
> justlookin320
> Hey I'm actually only 24 I made this account because I'm attracted to older women. Would you ever Fck a 24 year old
>
> > hey_by
> > when I was 24
>
> justlookin320
> Lol how bout now I'll make you feel like you're 24 again ;) you look amazing btw
>
> > hey_by
> > i already feel like i'm 24… and i find older men more attractive.
> > But thank you :)

Rose does not feel like she is twenty-four, but Cela has insisted she keep things light. This is the way of things now. Cela may as well have told Rose to take her brain out and put it to soak in a bowl on her bedside table. Rose knows wit, appreciates it, but insolence is hard to abide. It is only the twinge of flattery stirring somewhere in Rose's belly or her brain cells that saves the boy a tongue-lashing.

And for every one of those kinds of messages, there is one that baffles Rose.

> your conversation with propertyboy
> propertyboy
> hey there… were you drinking when the white dress photo was taken?
>
> > hey_by
> > you mean the pic of me with a drink in my hand??
> > : P

propertyboy
yes the one where you look hammered?

> hey_by
> well I was having my first drink of the evening... maybe you
> just don't like my look?

propertyboy
or that particular picture...

> hey_by
> okay?

propertyboy
actually I was looking for a classy lady but obviously I haven't
found one

Rose tries not to take these things personally. As she also
does when insipid men ask probing questions about personal
proclivities that she wouldn't even discuss with her sisters.

your conversation with buff_santa
buff_santa
I think you are a beautiful woman.

> hey_by
> and i like your taste so...

buff_santa
And I think you might be totally awesome :)

> hey_by
> and i can't disagree...

buff_santa
What amazes me is that you don't have someone.

> hey_by
> i keep finding someones... but i guess i'm more of a catch
> and release kinda person... never keep em very long : /
> but you shouldn't be so amazed... i might be a b***** in

person... you really have no way of knowing... i mean i'm not haha but you don't know that

buff_santa
That blows my mind. Do you keep meeting them here???

> hey_by
> why does it blow your mind?
> I've never met a man in a bookstore or a grocery store or a library.
> Here is just a macrocosm (if that's a word) of there... wherever there happens to be... I mean it absolutely gives people permission to be whoever they want to be for a little bit but it's fleeting if it's a facade, no different than the real world really except the machismo is heightened initially... so you're married?

buff_santa
why do you say that?

> hey_by
> your profile says not looking for a relationship or any kind of commitment... just assuming that's because you already have one

buff_santa
brains too :)))))

> hey_by
> so what the hell do you get out of being here????

buff_santa
I love my wife very much. I'm here for a good reason actually. Besides being lonely when I'm away for work.
I am a geologist and work in the woods a lot. The best way to find out when there is snow in the woods is to touch base with people in the area I will be visiting and ask them.
Actually I'm going to be deleting my profile here. Too much bullshit and disrespect. I'm a very discreet guy and respect women more than most of the assholes here. But I like you and would like to stay in touch but will leave that up to you. If you feel the same, send me a friend request on my facebook page. Hope you do. :)

hey_by
added the weather network app to your phone did ya???

Rose blocks him before she gets herself embroiled in complex explanations of how discretion does not equal respect and how, in fact, his discretion is nothing more than self-preservation. It is not Rose's job to fix every broken man on the internet. Not tonight.

your conversation with markymark
markymark
You have a beautiful smile. Come here often?

hey_by
thanks :)
when i'm single… usually about once a year :)

markymark
Single every year?

hey_by
haven't found one that lasted longer than that yet… haven't found "the one" i guess :)

markymark
Well hopefully I'll be making you smile two years from now :-)

hey_by
haha that's a really good comeback

markymark
It is very hard to keep females engaged here. Successful and fun conversation one day does not translate into a connection the next day. It is like Groundhog Day in here for me.

hey_by
yeah it's a weird alternate reality isn't it?
engagement is key though
i'll lose interest if a person can't make me smile every time we chat
probably not fair but nature of the beast i guess

markymark
I can make you smile every day but I need to be made smile also. It should be a two-way street.

> hey_by
> oh.
> i mean i honestly try to engage the other person too.
> that's why i end up with so goddamn many LOLs and HAHAHAs
> to be sure people get that i'm not being serious…the body language missing is a big piece too right

markymark
For years now I have preached that social media is the destruction of being social. I am very tired of adding the lol and : -) so people know my mood when I type something. Face to face is the only true way to know.

> hey_by
> i agree 1000%
> on the face to face being the only way to know i mean but social media is here to stay so how do we find a way to make it workable becomes the question right? I mean not that we need to find an answer tonight HAHA LOL :-)

markymark
HeHe this is true. We have the rest of our lives together to figure it out sure. lol It's a pleasure to be typing with you. I'm Terry. No pressure to tell me your name honestly : -) I'm off to bed. I will be here again tomorrow :- (Would love to make you smile again :-) lol

hey_by
Rose
Good night Terry
:- D

> markymark
> :- P
> 😊

After a week of chatting, Rose and Terry met for drinks, and it went very well. And it goes well for several months. And they are exclusive. Rose is supposed to bring him to dinner for Cela to meet him. She doesn't want to let Cela down, but Rose doesn't think she can take one more minute of it. Terry is a perfectly good man, but she cannot imagine turning in to him every night, a wastebasket full of tissues in the corner of her bedroom.

He wipes the tip of his bird with tissue, Cela. As soon as we're done. He keeps a box of tissues on his night stand.

Rose, that is normal. Normal people do that.

Oh Cela, please. If Luke did that we wouldn't have lasted anyway.

Everyone does it, Rose. Don does it.

Oh my god, Cela. I can't unhear that. Ew. Just ew.

Rose, get over yourself. You're acting like a child. You're just looking for an excuse.

Rose sticks her tongue out at Cela and mimics an uncontrollable shudder, shaking her shoulders and grimacing.

Not happening, Cela. Can't do it.

Cela rolls her eyes, disappointed that Rose refuses to make it work. Again.

I'll have good stories to tell though, Cela.

Facade

2010

Rose reclines in the chair, staring up into Dr. Long's face. She squints against the glaring light, glancing from the fingerprints on its chrome perimeter to his yellow eyebrows and wrinkled, steel-blue eyes, until the job is well under way. For a man who works with such precision, Dr. Long has shabby blond hair, and a leftover-hippie look about him. He wears navy deck shoes with leather laces left untied and a short-sleeved plaid dress shirt, thin lines of red and blue intersecting on a white background. The shirt puckers between buttons above a small paunch—which persists despite his twice weekly yoga sessions he chit-chats about—revealing white, hairless skin. He has a pale, freckled face and a skinny red moustache. He looks like an evening drinker. His assistant is young. She wears a hospital uniform—turquoise pants with a flower-print tunic.

So, Rose, I'll start your root canal today, and we'll make an appointment for a couple weeks from now to finish it. It'll let me implant the ceramic post I need, to rebuild a front tooth for you. The ceramic is bright white, so it won't show through the tooth like a metal post would. I swear Rose, you have the teeth of an eighty-year-old, I hate to say. I don't know what's wrong with them.

Dr. Long shakes his head. During the root canal, he will remove the pulp of the tooth and carefully clean and disinfect inside, then fill and seal the tooth with gutta-percha, before the final work is done. Dr. Long explains each step he will take in a low, soothing tone, like a grandfather shushing his baby to sleep.

The post will act as an anchor to hold the new tooth in place. Like this.

He turns to the adjustable side table at his right elbow, pushes the neatly aligned tray of tools slightly to one side, and uses the paper liner on the table to ink a crude sketch of his work. He draws the tooth and its root, arrows and x's pointing to the details he's explaining.

So this is the very tip of your root, right up here. It will be filled with cement. I'll drill into that and install the post. It'll stop about here, and then will extend down here. I'll rebuild basically a whole new tooth for you. It'll be lovely.

Rose wishes everything was so easy. Dr. Long turns from his drawing and slips on rubber gloves, like a second skin. Pulls the tool tray back in place, surveys it. Mirror, probe, tweezers, excavator, forceps, syringe.

He picks up the mirror and leans close over Rose as she opens wide. Pokes around with his fingers.

Feel that?

No.

Prods and pushes with the probe.

Feel that?

No.

He roots harder, sprays a hard stream of water into the fissure, droplets flying up and catching the light.

That?

I feel you doing it, but it doesn't hurt.

Rose doesn't know if he understood a word. Dr. Long straightens as he lays the water jet aside.

This is all dead here. Nothing alive. It's startling really.

That is exactly how Rose feels some days. She looks normal on the surface.

You said that about my teeth last time. You did fillings with no needle.

He scoots his wheeled seat to the counter and glances at Rose's chart. Shakes his head again. Pushes back to Rose and busies himself in her mouth.

We won't be doing this without a needle. Won't take that chance. I'll have to drill through what's left of your natural tooth—there's only a fragment really—and up into the root as far as I can. Don't worry, I'm leaving the old filling in place for now. I won't send you home looking like a hockey player.

Rose looks at this performer of miracles. Just build a new one of whatever is broken. If he only knew. If anyone only knew. Rose has taken good care of her appearance, but the visits with Luke are aging her. She feels the leap of time every October in the wall. She trusts Dr. Long. Her lips attempt a smile around his fingers, as she thinks about her secrets.

But no steak or nuts, or anything hard, for the next couple weeks. Only food as soft and mushy as you can handle.

Dr. Long lays his probe on the tray.

Okay, I'll do a liquid diet only. Vodka and cranberry for two weeks.

Rose makes no apologies to anyone for the Iceberg Vodka she keeps in her freezer, the Baileys in her pantry cupboard beside her pots and pans.

Okay, let's get a needle in you. That'll take a few minutes to take effect, and then we can get down to serious business here. This will only pinch. I promise.

Dr. Long inserts the needle, gently, leaning forward then back, as he removes it. Only a pinch. Rose doesn't feel anything.

I really don't know what the hell is going on with your teeth, Rose. The inside of your mouth is at least fifteen years older than you are. It's the damnedest thing. Don't worry, though. It will look just like your own. No one will be any the wiser.

Bed

I love you, Luke.

Luke mumbles as he turns over in the bed, burrowing deeper into sleep.

Ditto.

Rose stands watching Luke for minutes, or hours, her feelings balled together. She doesn't know what the knot in her gut means anymore. Life gets harder to manage every time she comes. Rose closes the door gently as she leaves, steps lightly down the stairs.

Muscle sinew bone. Muscle sinew bone.

Rose steps back through the living-room wall, into October.

Her head is on a pillow. She wakes to a clean slate, for two seconds. Then, *Luke*, like a neon sign, over there, off away in the upper left corner of darkness, behind her lids. The reality of the sign, of why the name is in lights, is like a flicker, before the word is flooded, swept up in the dread, the sign flashing now, in the time before her eyes blink open. And close. Refuse to open again. The bedroom looks like it did yesterday. When Luke was still alive.

Genes

2011

Rose learns that children who lose a parent before age eleven have a 50 per cent chance of developing mental illness. Fifty. Rose's aunt Jane—who gave her a card every year because their birthdays were a day apart—had a big house that was chock full of children. The house was riddled with craziness. She always had bad nerves herself, and many of her kids—who are much older than Rose because Jane is her mother's aunt—got the depression/anxiety/bipolar/manic-depressive gene and passed it on. Rose was not close to these cousins but felt she knew them because of Jane, and as she grew up, she wondered how a whole family could be so sick and how they managed to survive losing siblings and children. Rose had the presence of mind to thank god it was their family and not hers.

Although the exact cause of most mental illnesses can't be pinpointed, Rose's research shows that many are caused by a combination of biological, psychological, and environmental factors. Some mental illnesses appear to be related to the abnormal functioning of neural pathways that connect different brain regions. Heredity plays its part; it's common to see specific illnesses run in families. Susceptibility to mental illness is what is actually passed on through genes, but susceptibility doesn't necessarily result in mental illness. An important early loss, such as the loss of a parent, is a recognized psychological factor associated with the development of certain types of mental illness.

****

Rose sits in a small room at the Janeway Emergency Department, whose walls are pale pink and green. The shiny grey speckled floors run up the bottom edge of the wall to form a baseboard. There are two chrome chairs with black padded seats and backs, a hospital-bed table that raises and lowers by turning a handle at its end, and an intern who isn't quite sure how to get rid of this woman and her teenage daughter with the scowl.

The intern is wearing Crocs with tan-coloured footlets peeking over the top. She looks like a grandmother. Her body seems to apologize for the space it occupies. Rose wants to tell her she's worthy. Wonders how she got here. The intern questions Emily, determines that this is not a life-threatening situation, because Emily is not considering self-harm at this time, and tells them that she can be placed on a list for follow-up if they are interested. Rose apologizes to the young doctor.

I understand that this is not your fault. I already know the system way too well.

Thank you.

Don't thank me yet.

Rose is battling apathy in a white lab coat. Waging war on the calm decorum of the children's hospital and the young inexperienced students who are left to face the madness. Yes, she understands that it is not their fault.

You know, I get that this is not a priority for you. I get that. But we're not leaving this room, do you hear me? We'll set up house in here if we have to.

Mrs Tremblett, I don't think you understand.

Clipped, precise English. Devoid of the charm of any accent. Rose wonders if the doctors are nice to her.

No, I don't think *you* understand. We're not leaving here until we have an appointment to see a doctor this week.

I don't think we can do that. There's a waitlist.

Rose pounces on her timidity. Adds another cut to her wounds. Survival of the fittest and all that. Or survival of the one with the fittest mother. Whatever it takes.

Oh, we'll do it. We'll be the squeaky wheel. Because it's not normal for a tiny teenage girl to turn over bookshelves taller than herself. And to smash mirrors that I had to wrestle with to hang. My little girl. So you see, this is the most important thing in the world. And we're not going anywhere.

The intern stares at Rose, then leaves the room without another word. She stays away for a long time, eventually returning with a business card that has an appointment scribbled on it for Friday morning, with the head of Children's Psychiatry. Rose wants to pat the girl's hand. Wonders if she had a mother to fight for her.

Thank you, my dear. You have yourself a good day.

Rose bundles into her coat and whisks Emily out into the hallway, as she tucks the card safely away in a zipped compartment of her wallet. The intern stands still, until she hears the outer door swing open and shut. Then she herself leaves the cramped room and forces a smile to her face as she approaches another patient.

Rose spends the next months watching Emily's hatred grow for the head of psychiatry. Rose tries to get Emily to like her, then she tries to get her to at least tolerate her, then she tries to get her to at least go to her appointments. Because they need that doctor like an IV line.

Rose only found out when it hit her own little family that it wasn't just Jane's crew. Rose's own crowd just hides it better and is more fortunate than Jane's, not having it exposed in the obituaries of the Sunday paper. Between the genetics and the dead father, Emily didn't really stand a chance.

Janeway

Lying on the floor in the bathroom off the admissions ward at the Janeway Emergency in July, her cheek is conscious of the cool tiles, her eyes moving up to the curve of the toilet bowl, then running over the plumbing that is jutting out of the wall under the sink. Rose gives herself ten minutes to stifle screams and ask, *Why me.* She has to get up and go out there and face the fact that she yelled at the dog for pissing on the floor, and then yelled up the stairs at Emily to come clean it up, and she came, groggy and plastic-faced.

Emily heard her mother's voice, just as her eyelids were drooping, and she rose from the bed and followed the familiar sound.

Groggy and plastic-faced. Staring at her mother but not seeing her. Her feet seemed to be leading the way, but even they changed their mind, and Emily sat halfway down the stairs and said, "I'm sorry." *I'm sorry*, slurred.

Rose stared at Emily's face, stripped of everything that was Emily. Its edges and hollows puffed, rounded, the eyes like flat pebbles. Empty. Rose was paralyzed. She wanted Emily.

What have you done?

Pills.

What pills?

Dun-no.

What pills, Emily?

I don't. Know.

Go back and get the bottles.

Emily sat there.

Go back and get the bottles! We'll need the bottles.

Rose thanked god that Cela was visiting and sent Emily back up the stairs to get the bottles—sent her dying child back up the stairs—while she yelled to Cela to come help. They piled Emily into the front seat and Cela made Rose get out of the driver's seat and Rose wished for Luke all the way up Prince Philip Drive. Rose found it hard to look at her daughter's face when she was missing from it, and her eyes darted around and out the windows, looking for something to focus on. She leaned her forehead on the back of the driver's seat, behind Cela. Her mind screaming, screaming. She suddenly felt bad for the little rabbits that Luke used to hunt, innocent babies caught in snares.

Sometimes Rose's love is a frantic flurry of words and offerings. Sometimes it is like cymbals in her head. Rose has lived without Luke long enough that she has adjusted to it, and doesn't miss him or need him now. October is usually enough for her. But some things require more than one person. Some things require more than one heart.

Rose eases herself up from the bathroom floor, splashes cold water over her face, and pats her swollen eyes with government-issue paper towel. She pulls the heavy door open, feels the tug of resistance from the hydraulic door hinge, listens to the quiet *whoosh* before she heads back to the curtained bed that holds Emily. There is only one other patient inside tonight, so the ward is calm, and the women in uniforms, which are festooned with puppies or bunnies or clowns, bustle around Emily and Rose and Cela, creating chaos behind the curtain, in their attempts to soothe.

Youngsters. You don't know what they're going to get up to.

One of the nurses clucks as she brushes Rose's forearm with her fingertips.

She'll be all right.

Rose is certain this nurse does not require a response.

Another one is inserting an IV into the back of Emily's wrist. She prods the needle, to lead it where she wants it to go, pushing it to one side, pulling it back a little, then pushing it deeper under Emily's skin. Emily grimaces, but she is not aware that a needle has punctured her epidermis and is being taped to her arm. Needles make Emily dizzy. Even with all the tattoos. This nurse is all business, while the others appear to be bystanders. Rose appreciates her brusqueness. Appreciates that she is not distracted by the air of camaraderie the others offer.

Please step outside the curtain. I need to insert a catheter.

Rose clenches the white cotton drape and opens a narrow gap that she and Cela slip through. A hand on the inside closes it, and Cela and Rose stand frozen, murmurs and moans wafting through the flimsy veil. Rose has never had a catheter. She doesn't know what to do for Emily. She looks at Cela, but Cela doesn't know either.

The business nurse pushes out through the curtain.

Okay, you can go back in.

She motions them inside as she scurries away. She returns with a glass full of thick, grey liquid. It looks like molten ash. The nurse lays her hand on Emily's cheek and looks her in the eye, to make her focus.

This is charcoal. You have to drink it without throwing up, or you'll have to start over again.

Emily drinks a quarter of the glass, glances at the nurse, drinks some more.

You can take a little break. Give it a minute. Slow and easy.

Emily rests the glass on her leg, burps, takes a sip, drinks again. When the heavy business of soaking up hydrochlorothiazide, perindopril, and sertraline and getting her to pee, is well under way, a young male doctor with black hair pushes the curtain aside. He glances at his clipboard.

So Emily, how're we doing? I'm just going to ask you a few questions now that I want you to answer to the best of your ability. Nothing too hard.

The doctor fixes a smile and sits on the edge of Emily's bed, his clipboard resting in his lap.

What is your full name?

She looks at him, then at her mother.

It's okay, darling, just tell him your name. You remember it, don't you?

Emily Luke Tremblett.

Okay. What year is it?

It's twen... I think it's 2012.

Yes. Good.

Where are you?

Emily looks around her, at the busy uniforms, the bedpan on the side table, her mother.

I'm at the hospital.

She will be staying for the night. Emily is not to be left alone. She is not allowed anything that could pose a danger. These things are discussed in front of Emily, as if she is not there. As if she has not just proven that she is conscious. That she is still here. When the commotion settles, and Rose and Cela are left to sit with Emily and one nurse, Emily gazes at them with mounting recognition.

I s'pose they'll still let me have my birth control. I can't swallow that.

Cela half rises in her seat, then sits again. Confusion and panic flit across her face.

She's joking, Cela. It's a joke. She just gave up the pill. She switched to NuvaRing. She can't swallow that. It's too big.

Rose pats Emily's hand and beams, as if she is a kindergartner who has gotten her alphabet right for the first time.

Happy Birthday

Emily's favourite meal is baked macaroni. To the point that it has to be served at every function of any importance that she has any say in — including her birthday. And god forbid Rose alter the recipe. She must keep it simple. Rose mimics Emily's voice in a singsong as she pulls the steaming casserole from the oven.

Godsake. Don't add lobster or white cheese to the baked macaroni.

Rose doesn't remember when the macaroni became a party staple, but she knows that Emily was pretty young. Back then, Emily knew what she wanted. Knew who she was. When she was two years old and would fold her little body onto the living-room window bench, lie there quietly until Rose's attention waned, then hurl herself onto the hardwood. She was ensuring that she drew her mother's gaze back to her.

Emily is an atheist now, but as a child she'd toss her auburn curls across her back, the light from the window shattering them into browns and reds and golds, and she'd say, "Oh, Jesus gave me my highlights."

Emily loved to visit the salon, especially on Christmas Eve, when Rose let the kids open gifts after she'd sent the last customer on their way and locked the door. Emily still loves

Christmas because it's family time. She has taken so many pictures of everyone in front of Christmas trees, or around birthday cakes, or gathered on the patio, grinning at her standing behind the camera, being ridiculous—sticking her finger up her nose, or burping long and loud, or pulling her shirt up—to make them laugh.

Emily was seven when they moved to town for Rose to go to university, and eight when they moved back to Ferndale. When Maggie finished high school, they moved into the heart of St. John's, to live in a rambling old house that Rose fell in love with. Emily taught herself to love being the new kid at school and always dragged home a houseful of friends before the end of September. When Emily was in high school, she got into the piercings and tattoos and blue hair.

Emily's birthday celebrations range from gaggles of five-year-olds to family-only affairs. This year, Rose threw a carnival-themed surprise party in August. That she told Emily about in April. Over the spring and summer, Rose spent days in her bedroom, door closed and furniture pushed against the walls, creating backdrops to transform their home into a wonderland for a day.

There was a kissing booth where Emily collected thirty-eight dollars from her aunts and her cousins and her grandmother; three-foot-tall plastic flowers on every wall; a photo booth that took up the whole living room with a bureau full of costumes and props—hats, boas, and moustaches, umbrellas and outrageous sunglasses. The patio was festooned with more plastic flowers and birds and butterflies. There were bubble wands the size of walking sticks to wave. A ball toss with tent top and baskets of tennis balls. Prizes were tied to the rafters with twine. There were checker games and three-legged races and silver trophies, and there was joy spilling over the fences.

Rose told Emily the plan months in advance. Hoping that Emily would want to stay alive for it. And for the macaroni. Rose made it with elbow pasta, Cheese Whiz, Carnation milk, bread crumbs, and salt.

Thread

2014

Emily stitched her very first needlepoint piece and gave it to her mother. Emily is just finishing her hairstyling and aesthetician program, which Rose always swore Emily would only do over her dead body. Rose wants more for Emily. She doesn't like Emily's new boyfriend but gives him a lift to the graduation party and drapes her arm across his back for a picture, because she and her daughter have been through a lot together, and she is not about to let some little asshole get in the way of what they've worked so hard for. This too will pass.

Rose spent days combing the jewellery stores at the mall to find the perfect diamond studs for Emily that wouldn't also bankrupt her. Emily slips them into the second holes in her earlobes — below her industrial, whose barbell impales the cartilage either side of the top of Emily's ear. She's afraid she'll lose the petite carbon squares, perfected over a billion years of pressure, but she doesn't want to disappoint her mother. She's wearing the long black sheath that Rose found at Winners but didn't really expect Emily to agree to. The silver beading — little reflective rectangles punctuated with glass balls, like shiny exclamation points encircling her — cover the halter bodice and form a sash around Emily's wasp waist, the dark fabric hugging her before it swishes away at the tail. Rose chose it because her daughter did not attend prom and she wants to make it up to her. Emily loves the dress.

Rose drives to Michaels and buys a square white frame with a white mat. Abbey is the cross-stitcher in the family. She told Rose to get a self-stick mounting board for Emily's work, but Rose chooses a heavy paperboard and HeatnBond, for the "strongest bond possible," after consulting with the girl who comes to rescue her in aisle sixteen. There is more than enough in the Value Pack of heat-activated adhesive to do a couple practice runs on a pillow case, before committing embroidery to board.

Rose retrieves the ironing board from behind her closet door. It squeals as she releases the lever and lowers its legs. She lines up her supplies neatly on the plain grey padding—sharp scissors, pencil, cardboard, sticky backing, frame. She then removes the glass and sizes everything behind it, centring the picture before tracing careful straight lines around its perimeter. Rose lays the frame and glass aside and assembles the piece: places the material displaying a single word in black thread face down; presses it until it is wrinkle-free; positions the bonding agent, paper up, steam rising from the edges of the hot iron; peels the paper backing, flips the square, and sets it precisely on the hard board; repeats the process of bonding layer to layer. She reassembles the frame with its contents—square white wood, non-reflective glass, white mat, bonded embroidery, frame back.

Rose attaches 3M velcro strips to the back of the frame and to her living-room wall. Emily's artwork is centred above a table, to the right of a studio floor lamp. Rose surveys the project, presses her fingertips together like a church steeple. Navy-blue paisley on ivory fabric displaying *shit* in cursive.

Dave

September fifth was the last time Rose saw Dave. They'd spent the night at the Delta before he drove to Argentia to catch the ferry. Rose lingered in the parking lot, telling Dave to drive carefully with that old Harley propped up like that in the back of his pickup. "You don't know potholes till you drive that access road." When the first drops of rain fell, Rose said, "Okay love, this is it, I guess. Give me a hug." Dave stepped close and wrapped his arms around her. "This is not it Rose. It's not goodbye. I'll be back before you know it." Rose buried her head into his shoulder and hugged him tightly.

Every time Rose and Cela broke open a second bottle of wine together, they knew they were in for a night of solving Rose's man problems. Before Rose met Dave, she and Cela used to laugh about how Rose was too hard on men, how they didn't stand a chance.

You're doing it wrong, Rose. You don't need to look for someone you can spend forever with anymore. We both know you're not spending one day more than a year with the man. You never do. So just look for someone you can stomach for a year.

Rose would tease Cela about her good fortune. Cela has Don. Doesn't have to do the online dating thing like Rose.

Imagine, Cela, a man you've only known for a couple months, grabbing you by both ankles—right in the middle of it just grabbing you by both ankles—and lifting them up behind your ears.

Cela reaches for the wine bottle and tops up their glasses.

How do you think you'd feel, Cela? Not sexy, I'll tell you that. Because, you know, you're probably a little distracted because your left tit has somehow managed to get itself firmly wedged in your armpit and you're finding it a little hard to breathe. *Uhhhhhh*. Then he pushes harder. *Yeah, baby. Yeah. YEAH. Uhhhhh, holy shit*. And at the same time you're trying to wrangle your tit loose, you're also trying to keep your chin up so you don't look like Alfred Hitchcock.

Cela chimes in.

And suck your belly in so it doesn't double over itself in the middle.

Yes, and the more you wriggle to try to get your tit undone, the more excited he gets and the harder he pushes, until about two hours in he gives a great big heave and the tit comes flying out of your armpit and you're right relieved. *Ahhhhhh*.

Throwing her head back, Cela squeals.

And he moans back.

Yes. He goes *Ahhhhhh* even louder. And it's done. Not all it's cracked up to be, Cela. Not all it's cracked up to be.

The women clink their glasses together, then fall back on opposite ends of the couch. They decide that Rose will do a man the courtesy, now, of letting him know that he has one year, at the outside. If he can keep her ankles below her ears.

That was before she met Dave. Dave was different. They met for the first time in December at the Grapevine. He called her "dude," and they drank Coors Light together. They clicked. They talked about things that are not the weather or traffic or how Rose's mother's doctor supports her hypochondria. The hours flew even though they both had to work the next day. They strolled together up the sidewalk, filled up, proud of each other's goals and accomplishments and grandkids. Before Rose got home, Dave texted her to tell her what a great night he had and that he wants to keep in touch. One month later, there will be a handful of dates while he's in town for work and 229 emails exchanged.

When they hang out at their favourite pub—they have a favourite because this is still so new and Liam and Emily are still at home and Dave lives in company housing—strangers, a young man and then a middle-aged woman, comment on their obvious happiness and compatibility. A young guy high-fives Dave, and Dave asks Rose if anything like that has ever happened in the world before. He's laughing because she's lied through her teeth to these people about their history and said they've been together for twenty-eight years, but then she feels bad and goes to the woman's table and tells her the truth. The truth is that they barely know each other after a couple months but they cherish each other—Rose cherishes Dave, even though he's a mainlander.

When Dave tells Rose he wants to see some real culture, she takes him to the Crow's Nest on a Tuesday for a story-telling circle and it's new to both of them and it's amazing and she decides that it can't be so hard so she'll have a go at it and she puts her name on the list on her way back from the washroom. When it's her turn Dave looks a little stunned sitting there surrounded by World War II memorabilia and ships' bells and strangers who are sharing their table because the room is packed, but he scoots out to the edge of the bench to let Rose go, and she stands in the circle in the middle of the bar where couches and comfy-looking chairs have been arranged around a low table and a stool for anyone who prefers to sit while they share their stories of fantastic journeys and hockey games and strangers who became friends.

Rose tells her story of resettlement—how her mother took the cupboards from their abandoned house and hauled them across the bay and made them the centre of their new lives and over the years she painted them and covered them with wallpaper and painted them again. And Jesus is hanging on the wall watching them eat supper, wondering if he's in hell, and those cupboards could tell stories if they could talk.

Dave's expression is exactly the same as her father's the day he found out that she finally got her own salon. And his nose is the same too. And Rose and Dave are caught in each other's eyes and right there, among the crowd and the noise and the heat, Dave rises to his feet and he claps and he claps and he claps.

When Dave finds out her birthday is coming up, he asks for her work address to have flowers delivered and she says, "Oh no," but she secretly wishes he would find the address because everyone loves to get flowers at work, though she insisted no. And he wants to take her shopping, but she says, "Oh no, that would be too awkward." Not one to be thrown from a goal, Dave asks for one half-hour of her time on her birthday and he brings her a bag filled with their brief intimate history: a birthday card with a picture of a woman with obvious attitude and hair standing at crazy angles that reminded him of her mother making fun of her hair; a Montreal Canadiens keychain to herald her bullshit bravado about being a "sports buff" that dangled from her keys for the whole hockey season and led to many sheepish admissions to co-workers and acquaintances that she did not, in fact, know very much about the game; a bag of assorted single-serving chocolates to maintain the "voluptuous" curves, which is the best word she has ever heard coming out of a man's mouth; some one-ounce bottles of coconut rum that she likes to smuggle into movies to spike her Sprite; a gift card to her favourite scent shop because he loves the smell of her; a plastic potted bouquet of tulips that is also a lamp and still sports the Value Village price tag—an homage to her courage in going to Value Village for the first time with him and braving the penetrating eyes of people who might know her, as well as an homage to her gifts from Luke that were plastic and tacky that used to mortify her but that still hung on her walls—and somehow Dave knows that is the right thing to do. Rose sits in his truck with him on her birthday for one half-hour and she laughs and she cries.

When Dave tells her he's a gasoline addict, she has no clue what he means, but he looks so happy she still wants to hear all about his love affair with anything on wheels that is old and has integrity and runs on gas. He shows her a picture of his '71 Buick, the first car he ever owned, that both he and his son drove to their proms. He tells her about his old truck and his old van and his bikes. The thrill of sharing with her lights him up. The bike that he built himself after he found it in boxes of bits and pieces in some guy's barn and called his dad and bought it for five hundred dollars. He and his buddy spent ages putting it together. Dave talked to some other guy out West who knew about bikes, and when he mentioned that the serial number looked scuffed the guy got excited and Dave sent pics of it in the mail so the guy could confirm whether the bike was authentic. This was in the days before email and electronics and instant gratification. And Rose has no clue whether the '67 is the Harley or the British one or the one that Dave built, but she thinks it's the British one and she thinks that he built it and she looks at motorcycles differently now.

Dave requests she wear a little flowered sundress with buttons and fishnets and high heels—and she's willing to oblige him because he waited four months after they met before he booked a nice hotel room because he didn't want her to feel rushed—but the best she can do is a short black cotton button-front dress with orange geraniums and sleeves that can be rolled up and a pair of stilettos that she could never wear in public. Now he's rented an apartment for the summer in Georgestown because it is just around the corner from Rose, an old lady's dive that he calls "the condo." When he sees her coming, he whistles like a fifty-year-old voluptuous woman is god's gift to men. And they spend that evening and many more in harmony at the condo with its outdated furniture and its tiny television with no cable, laughing and talking and raising the neighbours' eyebrows late into the night and into the early morning hours.

The condo is sometimes the scene of debate about feminism and euthanasia and abortion, and they commiserate about poor old Latimer. Dave catches his breath at some of the things Rose says. He's surprised by her liberal outlook and her strong opinions, given her regular refusal to take a political position or even vote and her faith and whatnot. Rose finds out he is as passionate about things that matter as she is and he insists that Rose is too smart to be putting off her mammograms. Dave is adamant that his father would never have wanted to live like an invalid in a diaper and Dave doesn't ever want to be a burden and his daughter had an abortion that he wanted some say in—because he's her father, even though it's her body and he found out two years after the fact—and by the time the sun is thinking about coming up, Dave finds himself nodding when Rose says it's necessary for all people to be feminists and that there are no "women's" issues.

Dave slips a couple times when they're in a group and calls her wife, but they both know she'll likely never be his wife. She's sworn up and down that there'll never be another wedding and meant it—even though she's been known to tell a good-looking man that he looks exactly like her third husband and when the man gasps and asks how many husbands she's had, she says two. Dave got married once in the dead of winter in Western Canada far from home at Christmastime, but that was mostly to cheat the tax man and also to give his baby and future kids his name. And when he was drunk one night Dave said he never thought he'd ever get married again, but it'd be kinda cool to have all his grown-up kids in his wedding party. And when "wife" slips out they both ignore it, though he squeezes her hand a little tighter.

Things happen. September fifth was the last time Rose saw Dave. They'd spent the night at the Delta before he drove to Argentia to catch the ferry. Rose lingered in the parking lot, telling Dave to drive carefully with that old Harley propped up like that in the back of his pickup. "You don't know potholes till you drive that access road." When the first drops of rain fell, Rose said, "Okay love, this is it, I guess. Give me a hug." Dave stepped close and wrapped his arms around her. "This is not it Rose. It's not goodbye. I'll be back before you know it." Rose buried her head against his shoulder and hugged him tight, drew his scent deep into her lungs. She left it at that.

October is coming.

Nails

The young woman picks up each of Rose's hands in turn, loosely clasps the fingers in her own, runs her thumb absently across Rose's knuckles, rests each hand back on the black vinyl pad.

Do you like gel or acrylic?

Rose hasn't had artificial nails before, but she's finding it harder and harder to not feel like she she's old enough to be Luke's mother.

I have no idea. What's the difference?

Acrylic is better. I'll do acrylic.

Rose feels like her own mother just left her alone at school on her first day. Like she's in over her head.

Okay.

The woman immediately reaches into a drawer, withdraws an industrial-size nail clipper, and cuts Rose's paper-thin nails to the quick.

Your nails are like an old lady's. We'll start over.

Yes, Rose thinks. Every day. A flash of teeth as the woman pulls a white surgical mask over her mouth and nose, her eyes blinking. She reaches down out of sight and produces a drill the size of an electric toothbrush, with a sphere sandpaper tip, which she guides deftly across Rose's nail plates, raising a plume of microscopic cells that scatter and settle. Rose watches her push the cuticles back and snip away strands with a pincer. Nothing is easy.

The woman opens a translucent plastic box that is divided into two-inch square compartments, hundreds of oblong acrylic tips of varying widths contained within the box's walls. She squints at Rose's hand, picks a tip from the box, drops a spot of glue onto its back, and holds it securely in place where the frayed end of Rose's nail used to be. Over and over the woman does this. Rose's fingers don't know what to do. The woman pushes Rose's index finger down, or her ring finger up, out of the way, when they jut into her line of operation. They push back. Finally, Rose laughs at her hands, spread on the table with fingertips extending forever, like the pictures in the book of world records when she was a youngster.

Wait 'til I finish.

Okay.

Do you like them long?

Short. Please.

Rose doesn't want to look ridiculous. The woman takes a sharp scissor from a drawer and snips the nails back to a length Rose can live with, then picks up a small brown bottle, unscrews the cap, and dabs the brush full of primer — a concoction of methacrylic acid that will burn if it makes skin contact — on each of Rose's nails where they meet the plastic tips. Rose squirms a little in her chair as the woman anchors Rose's wrists to the vinyl pad again. Rose wishes she had asked her name but now she thinks it's too late. She wishes she knew how to prepare for things. The woman folds a crisp paper towel under Rose's hands, pours liquid acrylic into a glass bowl, and reaches for a crystal container filled with white acrylic powder, which she sifts and checks for lumps with the wooden handle of a brush she pulls from the tension arm of her lamp. She looks into Rose's eyes and cradles her hands in her own palm.

Just relax.

Rose looks back into deep brown eyes and exhales. Black hair skims the woman's shoulder as she tilts her head. The brush is held securely by the woman's thumb, veins prominent in the back of her hands like Rose's, as she repositions Rose's wrists and begins to fill the nails, lunulae to tips.

Are you going on vacation?

No. Yes. With my husband.

Nice.

The woman dips her brush in the pink liquid, wipes it against the rim of the bowl to remove the excess, then runs its tip through the heart-shaped jar of powder crystals until a small moist ball collects on the head of the brush, like a pearl. She places it on the nail of Rose's ring finger at the smile line, where the tip meets the nail, then smooths it nimbly over the entire surface, leaving a gentle curve in its wake. Rose is a natural hugger, and her fingers curl around the woman's hand as she moves from Rose's ring finger, to middle, to index. Rose's fingers move in unison with the woman's now, a touch here, a pressure there. Dip. Pearl. Smooth. Dip. Pearl. Smooth. The woman tweaks Rose's pinkie nail as she completes the final sweep of the nails, and buffs them to a supple finish with a flourish. She points to a sink that stands on a wall in Rose's peripheral vision.

Go and wash your hands. Then pick your colour. Something cheerful.

Rose washes her hands in warm water with a sudsy, cucumber-scented squirt from a bottle, and pats them dry on a white towel. She chooses a coral shade that is soothing, like peach schnapps, and settles back into her chair.

The woman murmurs her approval as she makes languorous strokes on each fingernail, base to tip. Then she places Rose's hands into two lighted plastic domes, like miniature Sprung Greenhouses. Warm and bright.

What does your husband do?

He's a fisherman. He's younger than I am now.

Rose stammers.

He's younger than I am.

Leaves the *now* off. The woman's eyes crinkle at the corners. She's used to hearing secrets. This one wants to be young forever.

Lucky you.

When the lights go off, the woman takes each of Rose's fingers again and with a soft, wet cloth, polishes the finish to a shine.

Your husband will like these for sure.

Rose stares at her hands. Veins rising like hills, the valleys crisscrossed by lines that amble off, fingertips like sunset. They smell clean.

I hope so.

Fractal

Rose is visiting with Luke. Her worlds are leaking into one another.

I just don't feel like it, Luke.

Rose rises and slips into the bathroom, turns the shower faucet to the wide red setting, lets the room steam before moving it back a notch and sliding her body into the spray. The force of the scalding water pelts against her sagging breasts, light splintering into rainbows caught in the droplets that splash up and away, bombarding her mouth and her cheeks as they escape into the air.

A girl Rose knew in high school lost her husband this morning, and Rose can't shake it. She closes her eyes as she turns away from the torrent, tipping her head up and back, water running down and over the sides of her head, engulfing her. She listens to the roar, like the ocean in her ears, as she sinks down and down into her thoughts.

> *Lie in a bed you didn't make.*
> *You will spend the rest of your life laughing in the arms of strangers.*

Ham baked until it sizzles, carved to keep the protective layer of fat on the outside, mashed potatoes whipped into a frenzy.

Perpetual loop.

Music is the universal language. Amelia Curran's band is introduced with some joke about the bass player's looks, but if he was ugly it would not matter.

Smarties are all about the hard, brightly coloured shell.

Twenty years will escape in a low moan.

Meringued lemon pie.

Try not to run people over with your car.

Liam looking down through the raw boards, trying to entice Maggie into Luke's big arms to bring her safely up the ladder.

Throwing dishes away.

You will dote on your grandchildren alone.

The boardwalk around Quidi Vidi Lake is a smooth shade of grey, weathered like an old woman's face. Footfalls on planks of uniform length and breadth that look like they were born that way. Shortened steps to accommodate the narrowed end of boards where they're cut to fit the angle of the turn. But the timber was never intended to be that way.

Christmas tree in March. Liam's balled fists and slouched shoulders.

Incessant tapping on the inside of skulls, like hailstones beating against old window panes.

Film developed that was sitting in a basket in a cupboard for eight years. Falling apart in a parking lot under the full glare of the sun.

Things you won't absorb that will come into
focus in the nighttime.
Love does not require a body.
Eaves on the newly finished house whiter than a
baby's first tooth. Serrated lines of dots and dashes
like Morse Code, extending into peripheral vision.
Lying in bed staring at the ceiling.
Fresh meat loves salt.
You will pour yourself out. You will not find him.

Luke opens the shower door and steps in.

Are you crying?

He hugs her as she slouches against him. Luke holds her up, water running into his eyes and his ears.

Judy's husband died this morning.

Rose never really knew her. Knows her intimately. Now.

Rose dresses and leaves while her hair is still wet, the sound of the water splashing on Luke's skin following her downstairs, echoing as she steps back through the living-room wall, into October.

Shoes

Rose stares down at her bare feet. For the life of her, she can't imagine why she has no shoes. She can't remember where she leaves anything. Rose sits on the floor, takes Luke's black dress shoes in her lap, and runs her fingers back and forth over the laces. She lays the shoes neatly back on the floor, stands up, slips her bare feet into them, and walks out the door, gripping the soles with her scrunched toes to keep them from slipping.

After a long drive from Ferndale, Cela pulls the car up to the front of the church, steps out and opens the door for Rose.

Wait here, Rose. Abbey is pulling in there now. She'll just be a minute.

Rose tilts her head skyward and takes in grey stone as high as she can look without losing her balance.

The Basilica is built of grey limestone and white granite quarried in Galway and Dublin, and sandstone from St. John's and Kellys Island. It is 260 feet long and its towers rise high into the air, containing nine bells between them. The St. John Bell, in the East Tower, was the largest ever cast in Ireland, and won a gold medal at the Dublin Exhibition of Irish Manufacturers in 1850. The steps span the entire front of the building, with handrails spaced along their width to guide the faithful inside. When it was finished in 1855, the Basilica was the largest church in all of North America.

As Cela and Abbey hurry toward her from the parking lot, Rose wanders up the steps, into sanctuary. She is standing just inside the massive doors, waiting to be told what to do, when they catch up and Cela slips her hand into Rose's. Entering the church feels important. Holy elegance.

Rose's eyes are pulled to the ornate high altar at the far end of the aisle, and upward to the magnificent ceiling, whose shape reminds Rose of the hull of an overturned ship.

The ceiling design, dating from 1903, consists of twelve raised panels in a circle at the intersection of nave and transept. The circle's circumference is two hundred feet. The panels have elaborate floral designs and contrived decorations, each one dedicated to a special virtue of the Virgin. There are six pendant drops embellished with a profusion of gold-leaf highlighting. Sunlight filters in through twenty-eight stained-glass windows taller than houses, which sit high up in the white walls; the jewel-toned designs of the Fifteen Mysteries of the Rosary were fashioned by Irish, English, and French craftsmen.

Rose's eyes drop again to floor level. The church is full but the aisle is empty. There will be no droning incantation over caskets, no incense wafting to heaven and burning the eyes out of everyone unfortunate enough to be seated in the front pews. Rose wonders where everyone supposes the souls are, and what the priest's job is now anyway, without bodies to bless and perform rituals over.

Rose surveys the crowd, then feels a hush in the air as heads turn and look her way. She scans the sea of kneeling bodies and her eyes stop. Wayne. Luke's best friend. He is crouched on a wooden kneeler, in the middle of a pew about three-quarters of the way down the aisle to the left. She catches his eye. He nods and tries to smile. Rose walks toward him without breaking eye contact. Wayne watches her approach, then rises and manoeuvres his way across the sea of people in the pew, walking on toes and mumbling, "Excuse me." He steps into the aisle and holds his arms wide with outstretched hands. Within reach of him, Rose hesitates. Wayne steps forward and wraps her in his arms. In the centre of the aisle, he holds her, their bodies aligned, both quivering, and she nestles her head into his shoulder. Wayne shushes in her ear and runs his flat palm down the back of her hair. He feels like a piece of Luke to Rose. When she can't stand the touch of him anymore, Rose lets go and continues down the aisle.

Cela walks behind her and eases her into the second pew from the front, on the right, with the rest of the family, and steps in past her. Rose sits on the edge of the pew. No interest in "Thy Will Be Done." She looks around. There must be every eye colour in the world here. So many eyes. A short, stout woman, with a familiar face and freshly brushed blond curls, is sitting a few pews behind her. Rose slips from her seat, heads back up the aisle to the woman's pew, reaches across two people blocking her way, and hugs her, throwing them both a little off kilter. The woman is the skipper's sister-in-law, who has come to the salon for years, but Rose, in her absentmindedness, has mistaken her for his wife, who is, of course, sitting in the front pew.

As she straightens herself, Rose watches a man approach, shimmering in the light streaming down from the windows. He stops in front of her. Rose remembers his face from the fish plant. He looks different in a sports jacket. He is very tall. He reaches for Rose's hand and shakes it firmly.

Hello, Rose. Remember me? Bud.

He owns the plant. He was not worried.

Thank you for coming, Bud.

Cela appears behind Rose again and herds her back to her seat as the service begins. One of the largest pipe organs east of Montréal, with sixty-six stops and 4,050 pipes, almost two pipes for each person who can be seated here, churns out music that swells and rises, the melody lifting to the rafters until the flowered panels drive the chorus back down again. It moves outward over the congregation in waves, before crashing upon white walls, only to rise to the rafters again. The choir sings along.

Rose sits through "Be Not Afraid" until it becomes unbearable, glances over her shoulder to see how far away the door is, steps out of the pew, turns her back to the archbishop at the altar, and runs in a halting gait. She runs past 322 pews without looking into any of the faces. She does not look at the skipper's wife or his sister-in-law, she does not look at Wayne, she does not look at Bud.

When she reaches the vestibule, Rose does not stop. She pushes all of her weight against the heavy panelled door, until it heaves outward and she plunges into sunlight. Rose gulps fresh, stinging air, filling her burning lungs with oxygen, and stumbles down the wide limestone steps, in the oversized shoes.

R Is for Rose

2014

Maggie gave Rose a pink book for Christmas. *What I Love About Mom*. Fifty sentences, with blank spaces she filled in:

1. I love your _smell_ .
4. I love when you call me _darling_ .
6. I'm thankful I got _your optimism_ .
18. If you were a superhero, your super power would be _bright light_ .
26. I love that you encourage me to _do whatever I'm doing_ .
31. I owe you an apology for _all the times I am mean to you_ .
47. You have the most beautiful _intentions_ .
50. I wonder if you know how _comforting you are_ .

Rose hugs the book, then turns back the pages.

38. If you wanted to, you could easily be _satisfied_ .

Satisfied. Rose doesn't know what satisfaction is anymore. She can't even settle on a signature *R*. For a while, Rose made her *R*s by forming a loop, like a raindrop, with a perfect circle attached, and an elegant half loop for a leg. It looked composed, but it was her mother's *R*, borrowed from school forms and the writing on birthday cards, and she couldn't keep up the pretense for long.

Handwriting analysts are said to be capable of producing a personality profile by examining the characteristics of an individual's handwriting. Some practitioners claim that beyond personality traits, many things are revealed, including health issues, morality, hidden talents, and past experiences.

The pressure that Rose applies to her handwriting indicates that she is healthy and forceful with high emotional energy. The right slant of her words means she responds strongly to emotional situations and is caring and outgoing—her heart rules her mind. The dot of her *i*, high above the stem and to the right, says that she tends to act hastily, has an active imagination, and focuses on tiny details instead of the big picture. The long stroke of her *t* indicates that she is determined, enthusiastic, and stubborn. Rose's signature has changed many times over the years, but the *R* remains unsatisfying, a thorn in her side. And Rose herself is always in flux, trying on jobs and houses and relationships, then sloughing them off like dead skin. Nothing fits.

Emily was seven when Rose decided she couldn't wait a day longer to go back to school. Rose dropped out of high school in grade eleven. Never returned after Christmas. Not even one call from the school to see where she was. Rose was smart, too smart for her own good sometimes, and she was saucy too. And the principal, Brother Williams, was at his wit's end trying to counsel a teenage girl with a rebellious streak, too big for her small town and the small expectations attached to her, and raging at her world. She'd never opened a textbook in her life but always made honour roll. And then she was out of his hair.

The first time Rose walked across the stage at Memorial University, she wore a long-sleeved black dress under her gown, and black patent-leather, pointy-toed shoes with a skinny ankle strap that flattered her leg. She wished that Luke was sitting in a chair next to the kids. He would have ignored the instructions to the audience, to hold their applause until the last graduate had walked across the stage. Luke would have risen from his seat and shouted her name. *Way to go, Rosie! I knew you could do it!* Rose believed in Luke's love, and the degree, and the shoes.

Rose goes through changes like other women change their lipstick. She bounces from Placentia Bay to Topsail Road. And back to Placentia Bay again, then to Monkstown Road. And she dates — Ron, Don, Roy, John — they all have the same name, Cela says.

Before Rose walks across the stage a second time, she already has a job with the fisheries union. For convocation, she wears a sleeveless summer dress, also black, and a pair of sturdy suede flip-flops. Her hair is big and meticulously messy, each layer flipped in a different direction. It sweeps her shoulders and the large silver hoops in her ears. Rose looks like she has her shit together.

But she is reminded that she does not have it together every time the *R* flails across the page, out of sorts, like the pieces of her that are still scattered among the debris of the *Elizabeth Coates*. Rose is afraid to be satisfied.

Thin Air

Rose works at the union with a woman whose daughter disappeared. Not a trace. The pink plaid shirt and grey jacket she wore tumble in the woman's dreams, swooping and somersaulting like kites with their strings cut away, gone to wing. The woman rolls from her belly to her back, her back to her belly, her belly to her back, the blankets twisting around her, pinning her down. When morning comes, the woman puts one foot in front of the other. Her whip-straight hair is dark and shiny as a crow, and the wide smile she perfected in her mirror—white white teeth behind crimson lips—never wavers.

Rose grits her teeth as she settles into a rear seat in the Dash 8 on her way to Labrador for meetings, gripping the armrests for takeoff to keep her fists from clenching. Suspended in air, her insides bottom out, like walking through a cemetery alone at night. Seventeen tons of metal pierce the clouds—no more than a gannet breaking the surface, in the grand scheme of things. Rose feels tiny as she is hurtled into another world, topsy-turvy.

Levelling off at seventeen thousand feet, a new layer unfolds. She releases her hold on the armrests, relaxes into her seat, and stares out the porthole at the drifts of cloud banks like an expanse of frozen ocean, mounds of snow dispersed along the craggy surface as far as she can see. No man-made structures — no roads, no houses with people behind drawn curtains, no fences hemming it all in. There is a stark calm. Arctic-bright light. Rose wouldn't be surprised to see a polar bear slouching toward the plane. Extending high above the cloud ceiling below her, blinding clear sky causes Rose to squint toward the white sun sitting on the eastern horizon.

Rose catches glimpses of black, green, blue. Sky and ground. A hole in the cloud underneath the plane opens wide, like the corner has been ripped off the edge of the sky, exposing the world below. World layered upon world. Rose feels as if she might fall back to Earth.

Gazing down at the land, its topography of natural and human scars, Rose thinks of Emily's scars. Of her piercings and tattoos. The earth is pitted with rivers and streams, valleys and dams, buildings, farms, roads running in parallel lines. Fawn-coloured square of a quarry, its delineation severe against the surrounding greens that blend into a single shade. Aftergrowth marking people's intrusion into forest, scattered yellow dots of deciduous trees clustered along gashes of highway, like pushpins on a map. The earth wounded and healed a thousand times.

The only straight lines were put there by humans. Dark green hills are smudged with grey, black lakes and ponds bordered by dirty brown shores, rivers snaking like varicose veins, one a serpent with an arrow head. All irregular shapes with uneven edges. Rose dozes off.

She descends a stairway through cloud cover, into her living room, which has a street running through it, and a bathroom on the far side of the road. The zebra-print walls are shrouded in fog. Very little traffic; a blue Camaro cruises past, before a motorcycle shimmies up the road, so slowly Rose worries it will topple onto her coffee table. The driver looks like Luke, but Luke knows Rose would never want him riding a bike. Rose yells to him over the growl of the engine as he goes by, her finger pointing and waving toward him.

You forgot to turn your headlight on.

The driver slows to a dead crawl, takes a sharp left turn around the bathroom corner, goes out of sight. Rose crosses the street and rests her hand on the facing of the bathroom door, waiting. Listens to the guttural snarl as he comes into sight again, back into her living room, and stops. He draws a gun, balancing himself and his bike with both feet, extends his arms in front of him, joins his hands, cradles the revolver. Rose ignores the chirping birds on the telephone wires hanging above her from the ceiling. She makes a quick step to duck into the bathroom, out of harm's way, when she catches a glimpse of Emily for the first time, out of the corner of her eye. Emily is sitting cross-legged on the floor, watching *Law and Order*. Rose lowers her hand slowly from the bathroom doorway, eases sideways, one step, one step, one step, her back to Emily. Positions herself between her daughter and the biker, becomes the middle point of the line separating them. Rose bristles to her full height. Faces the biker squarely.

Rose stirs restlessly in her seat, opens her eyes and peers out the window again. She wonders if what she sees is what's real. Wonders about reality. From a distance, everything is deceiving. Motion is suspended in the space between the worlds Rose is straddling. Like time standing still. Whitecaps on rivers like wisps of hovering cloud. Ripples on ponds like zigzags scribbled across a page. Waterfall still as a photograph. Sunshine is the only movement discernible to the eye, running like liquid mercury poured from the sky, bouncing from one body of water to the next. It reminds Rose of the shimmer on the reflective, crunchy fabric she had sewn into a costume for Emily, the iridescent glimmer of her mermaid tail.

Goosebumps rise on Rose's arms as the ground hurtles past below her, closer, time catching up. The airplane heads out over water, out over the edge of Newfoundland—a sheer wall of dry earth dropping away to the ocean, pocked with boulders the size of cars and snarled tree roots like massive veins, the island ripped from its origins, its wounds scabbing over. The plane dips and turns back toward Cabot Tower, toward land. Rose thinks about the water from when she was little, when she could see bottom. All the pretty greens.

When Rose was ten years old, she would lean her chin on the gunwale of her father's boat, looking at the rocks on the bottom of the shallow harbour. The rocks, spotted with lichens, turned shiny turquoise and teal shades with the sun's reflection. Rose loved the water, but it scared her when she could see bottom. She was scared to death of drowning. Never afraid coming down through Paradise Sound, in water so rough that the boat smacked off the waves like a baseball cracking on an aluminum bat. So rough Rose didn't dare lean over the side, or she'd be swept away. The waves were an impenetrable black, so there was nothing to see anyway. Her poor old father was frightened to death the lot of them were doomed. Rose and Cela and Abbey corralled into the bow where he could see them, grinning from ear to ear, salty hair plastered to their freckled faces, Rose not yet grown into her front teeth. Rose never gave one thought to drowning then. Only thought about it when she could see bottom. All the pretty greens.

Rose peers down onto the tracts of earth rushing by. The earth yields clusters of trees that yield straight lines subdividing the land into neighbourhoods that yield rows of houses like dominoes. Rose shifts her focus and the wing of the plane comes into view. The wheels drop and the trees rise. The landing gear always startles her, appearing much sooner than she expects, when transport trucks are still Dinkies on the ground.

Dogberries are heavy on the trees. As they make landfall, Rose peers up through the small window. It is the same sky but she feels a shift. Rose scans the cabin. Eighteen people. The rectangle above the adjoining seat says *No Smoking*. Tiny squares of weak light cast a pall over the group. In 15B a white baseball cap above a neat beard and a small silver hoop in the left ear. A single newspaper is folded, jackets and backpacks are scooped from underneath seats.

Rose takes up the rear of the passenger line, shuffling forward to deplane, laptop bag full of grey file folders weighing on her shoulder, one foot in front of the other. She gives the co-pilot–cum-flight-attendant a wide smile—white white teeth behind pale lips—the smile she perfected in her bathroom mirror.

The Girl in the Red Sweater

2015

Six thirty p.m. It is a frosty evening as Rose drives past her own house with the *For Sale* sign in the front garden. The house is alive, Rose's cinnamon sticks simmering in the kitchen and light shining from all its windows. There is a girl, a woman really, standing in the dining room, angled arms raised above her head, crossed at the wrists, stretching languorously. Rose imagines the nub of the girl's sweater, close, blood-red wool, tightly woven, sleeves a quarter way up the bent arms, loose turtleneck collar skimmed by a dark bob, blunt bangs capping her brows. Smiling into the face of a man whose back is to the window. Looking like she owns the place.

Harris Cottage was built in 1833, set back on Monkstown Road, with a five-sided porch, the only porch of its kind in Georgestown. William Harris, master builder, created a more modest home for his own family than many of the houses he constructed for the merchants in St. John's. It is one of the few structures to survive both of the great fires, its location deliberately chosen to avoid the downtown core, where buildings clung to each other, cannibalizing their neighbours when the flames came. It has always worn the brightest yellow clapboard, dory-green trim, crimson accents, in a sea of sober colour. In the early nineties, during a facelift to restore its original character, replacing cedar shingles and rotted boards, a baby's high-heel laced boot was retrieved when a section of wall was removed.

Rose saw Harris Cottage for the first time in the winter of 2004. The house was chilly, but it was the dead of winter and Rose was impressed with its ability to hold what little heat eked from the radiators. It had three fireplaces and remnants of a fourth, with dead embers still lying in the grates.

On the night Rose and the kids moved in, Cela and Don brought fried chicken, and they ate on the varnished, two-hundred-year-old pine floor of the master bedroom, the only room fit to have food in. The kitchen sat at the back of the house, stretching its width, flanked either side by additions that housed a laundry room and a walk-in pantry. It had a short stretch of orange oak cabinets along part of the far wall to the left, and a dilapidated refrigerator in the opposite corner by itself, a container of something still pushed to the back of its metal shelf. There was shamrock green linoleum, its underside a quarter inch of what looked like compressed sawdust backed by jute. It was gruelling to pry up, but beneath it were the original floorboards, ingrained with patches of old scraps of newspaper from New York, one dated August twenty-first, with the year missing. Emily's birthday. Rose lacquered the dark wooden floor, paper and all.

Once, on a bright summer day, as Rose cemented stone tiles in place over the crumbling concrete that was the front step, two old couples stopped on the sidewalk. One of the women had grown up visiting her uncle in this house, and what a lovely job Rose was doing too, in keeping it up. She told Rose about winter mornings in front of the fireplaces, when the coal was plentiful, and before long, four strangers were squeezed together with Rose in her front porch.

As Rose turns the creaky knob and the strangers pile into

the front hall, the glass of the transom window glints, spilling shards of colour onto the narrow staircase before them, its softwood treads dipping at the centre from nearly two centuries of footsteps. The old woman's eyes follow the light's path, peering up the stairwell at the ghosts of memories permeating the house. She is back home from the States and what luck to have stumbled upon Rose in the front garden. She is a Harris, and Rose's family is only the second to own and live in this house.

The large living room is swathed in zebra-print fur, its long wall lined from floor to ceiling with oversized gilded mirrors, some only leaning against the wall because they are too heavy to hang. A square coffee table — big, chunky, distressed — that Rose bought the year Luke died, sits at the centre, with linen couches, silver tables, a fireplace with blackened bricks and white embossed wood radiating from it. The old woman reaches out, her hand grazing the plush wall.

They shuffle into the dining room, whose chandelier — all shiny chrome filigree and glass teardrop pendants — is corralled inside a circle of wooden mouldings. Rose stole the wood from under her aunt's shed, where it lay after being rescued from the rubble of the church in Great Paradise. Inside the circle, printed on cotton paper, are the names of all Rose's family, living and dead, who came by blood or marriage. Maggie, Liam, and Emily are in the centre, around the chandelier's base. Beyond the moulding, the ceiling is covered in black-and-white family photos, printed on the same cotton paper. The old woman's hands flutter to her lips.

Your very own Sistine Chapel.

The stone tiles kept Rose in the front garden for much of the summer, and there was always someone stopping to talk to Liam's dog, and then feeling obliged to say hello to her as well. Harley held court from a tree stump, where he sat as still and grounded as the house itself. One day a man stopped and complimented the tiles, then told her he was making a movie and her house would be perfect. He knew the house from growing up in the neighbourhood and the overgrown back garden—he was nice about it and called it rugged and wild—would be ideal to film a harrowing scene, where a cat is put down in the woods.

The crew came at seven thirty and stayed until well after dark, the house bustling with impromptu sound stages, dressing rooms, and dozens of people. Liam was responsible for overseeing the comings and goings. They asked to pull the kitchen range away from the cabinets, to use the outlet, and Liam said, "Sure, if you sweep up the mouse shit." They set up a buffet in the driveway for the actors and crew, and the people and the food and the noise spilled onto the sidewalk and street. When they packed up, and left Rose and Liam to rearrange their tables and chairs and to sweep away the leftovers of the day, Liam said, "Mom, there must be a quicker fuckin' way to kill a cat."

Once, when the back garden was still an overgrown tangle of ferns and mile-a-minutes and maple trees gone wild, they danced on the sidewalk, during a going-away party for Maggie and her boyfriend Rick, who Rose loves like her own. None of the neighbours complained, and they wished them well and hoped their flight was uneventful. They came running back home from Alberta before Christmas, and Maggie tumbled into Rose's bed at three o'clock in the morning. Rose and the house hugged her tight. And when the back garden was tackled and tamed enough to build a patio and lay some heavy sods, through which the mile-a-minutes still poke, they danced out there instead.

And then Rick had to dig a hole under the biggest maple tree, tears dripping onto the fresh earth. For five days, Liam had walked the neighbourhood with Harley, as often as Harley wanted to go, stopping to say hello to strangers, which was not Liam's way, but everyone knew Harley, his colouring like a beagle, his shape and bearing like a miniature greyhound. They strolled while Harley sniffed every bush in Bannerman Park, absorbing memories, and cocked his leg slightly to dribble on fence posts. Liam slept on the living-room floor when Harley couldn't climb the stairs anymore, a blanket covering both their bodies, until he had to call the vet and tell him it was time. Harley's collar still lies on Liam's night stand.

Rose dusts and lays the collar back when potential buyers are coming to look at their home. She replaced the zebra print with linen-coloured burlap wallcovering, to help the house sell.

Rose is leaving. She is moving to a white house—white walls, white ceilings, laminate floors. Cela asks Rose why she's leaving another house behind.

Like Trudeau says, Cela, because it's 2015.

It's the only answer she has. A white house with white walls and white ceilings is clean. Like a new sheet of paper. She's poured herself into Harris Cottage, but it still wants so much. Maggie says it's been her mother's partner for the last ten years.

The summer of 2014, when Rose used her holidays to paint the house, she was struck by a realization—nine gallons of yellow, four gallons of green, and two gallons of burgundy paint, applied with an extension pole, balancing unsteadily on the porch roof to get to the eaves, overreaching. She couldn't do this anymore.

The girl in the red sweater stretches her neck back, gazing at the people on the ceiling, as she lowers her arms.

Rut

Easing the strap off doesn't help. Decades of support have made a permanent impression. Rose slides both hands behind her back, unhooks the clasp, and slips out of the bra, dropping it to the floor. She massages the indentation in her shoulder. Her right thumb creeps down the slope, into the valley, up the other side.

Rose watches her hand in the floor-length mirror as it moves, skimming her nipple. She catches the areola between index and middle fingers. Squeezes. Feels the nipple react to the touch. Sees it harden. She teases it with the fingertip of her pinkie. Three babies, the satisfying latch of their mouths, the milk inoculating them against infection, helping their immune systems develop. Rose slips her hand under the breast, cups it, her fingers splaying to hold it close, apologizing for complaining of the heaviness.

Rose's bosom held her heart when it was raw, when it hurt her to breathe. Twenty-one years later, she is sometimes finished her shower before she remembers.

Rose's breasts have longed for Luke's touch and been mollified by her own. And they have caused Rose to panic, a nurse examining them and hesitating. The nurse, Marion, talks in a soothing voice as she writes and makes markings on her diagram. "This is what will be sent to your doctor. See." She touches the paper gently, pointing. The same fingers that hesitated on her breast. "I'm indicating it here. Upper right quadrant, at ten o'clock. Twelve centimetres from the nipple."

Time ticks as Rose waits to see the doctor. She begins to dream. Or remember her dreams. She is dreaming about Luke. Her cellphone rings. Emily calling from her bedroom.

Can you come sleep with me?

Rose had just smiled at him. He smiled back, lopsided. His cheeks are fuller than she remembers, and peppered with freckles. Rose gets up and goes down the hall to Emily's room for a little chat. Quiet voices.

I was just in the middle of a visit with your dad.

Oh, sorry Mom.

No, don't be sorry. I probably wouldn't remember it in the morning if you hadn't woken me. He must have popped by just to see how you're doing.

Do you believe that stuff, Mom?

Oh, I don't know what I believe. But he hasn't visited me in a dream in twenty years.

He visits me now, Mom. I dream about him lately.

What do you dream?

Oh, nothing really. He just introduces himself and says he's so happy to meet me. Has on that green T-shirt he's wearing in the picture you have.

What else happens?

Nothing. It's like one of those dreams that you have the same over and over. He just reaches out.

He reaches out.

Yep. Just reaches his arms out for me to go to him.

Rose gives her shoulders a shake as they hunch.

Chilly in here.

Rose is surprised that Emily is dreaming about her father after all these years. She's never dreamt about him before. Luke coming while she's asleep, coming to see Emily in her sleep.

While Rose waits to hear from her doctor, time settles to a semblance of normal, but she is bothered. Rose keeps going back to the nurse's words, wondering if she will ever be able to go back to before she heard them. She threatens to cut off her breasts if they turn on her, if they ever even think about the C-word. Rose and her breasts are spared, this time.

Rose focuses on the mirror again, gazes at her hands slipping down her sides, following the curve of her waist, resting at her hips, gravitating to her stomach. She glances up, looks herself in the eye. Stares at a face that she's taken credit for over the years, as if she really had anything to do with its arrangement. Pretty enough for its age, but older than it should be. Her eyes fall back to her belly, the extra ten pounds. Rose lived so close to the abyss in the year after Luke died, drowning herself in food and wine, trying to ease the pain. She started eating at the food court. When she ate ice cream she could hear passersby think, *You wonder why you're so fat.* When she ate salad or a sensible sandwich she could almost hear them whisper, *As if that's what you eat when you're at home.*

With all the news coverage of the accident, strangers kept sending Rose money in sympathy cards and she swears she spent the whole six thousand dollars on Jersey Butter Toffee and poutine. Cela would get Rose tipsy and they'd take silly pictures together, and they'd laugh but they never talked about her weight. Until Rose decided she had to get herself together and take control of the scale. Rose still has the hunger, but she doesn't take it so literally anymore. Food and wine do not quench it. The bit of pudge now doesn't bother her unless it starts to sneak well past the ten. And she eats her Häagen-Dazs in private.

Rose kneads her belly with her fingertips, turning slightly to her left to size up the side profile. Her hand inches lower, grazes the stubbled hairline, comes to rest. Rose was surprised the first time that it wasn't itchy as it grew. Luke didn't know what to think of it. "I grew up when it was all about the bush, Rosie." But he was game. As long as Rose kept a patch on the little rise above her vagina. "Don't want you to look like a child." Sometimes Rose wishes the hair was thick, to sink her fingers in and pull when she lies awake all night, waiting for October.

Rose tells Cela maybe she'll grow it back and dye that purple too. When she sold the house and moved into her white walls with white trim, Rose felt like something was missing. Like she'd left her personality behind. So she gave herself a pixie cut and dyed her hair purple, the colour of the irises that grew in the bog behind their house in Great Paradise.

Rose doesn't mind wanting a man, but she thinks that needing one is a sign that something's wrong. Rose is not good at relationships. She doesn't make plans anymore. Happiness is not some big solid block. Rose used to have a relationship with god, but she knows she can't change one goddamn thing by kneeling down.

She has spent twenty years waiting for Luke. Rose follows her hand in the mirror as it returns to her shoulder, massages it, pulls the indentation taut between index and middle fingers, trying to smooth away the rut.

Abracadabra

2015

Rose goes back to work before the healing is complete. The bruises under her eyes are beginning to fade to yellow but the edges further along her cheekbones are pink stains rimmed in grey, taking so damn long to disappear. Everyone whispers. Both eyes. Rose's girlfriend comes into her office and closes the door.

What's going on?

Nothing, Kris.

Rose.

I swear to god, Kris. Nothing. You know me better than that. I just had a little injection.

Are you sure?

Swear.

Are you sure you're sure?

I'm not even dating anyone, much less letting a man put his hands on me.

Kris exhales and she squints into Rose's eyes before folding her into a hug.

I couldn't see it honestly, Rose, but couldn't imagine what else it'd be. You didn't say anything.

Well, I didn't really feel like announcing it to the world. I mean it's not a big deal. Just a little pick-me-up.

No big deal trying to keep up with time. Rose knew what she was getting into when she started the visits. That they would cost her. But it's like everything—you don't really know until you know. Until you see the wrinkles and grey hair and wear and tear on your body and your mind. Then it's too late. There's no rewind button. She traded time. She knew what she was at. Luke was always worth it. But now she has to cover up the fallout, and she's only touching the surface. Like Cela used to say when they had the salon, "I'm a beautician not a magician." There's only so much Rose can expect. The best she can do is control her weight, colour her hair, ignore the hurt in her muscles and her bones. And now Botox. But there's no magic.

Lacey says, "Rose, you are by no means old, you just have prematurely aging skin. We can fix you right up. Make this practically vanish." Lacey swishes her hand in front of Rose's face. She calls Botox a medicine, but all Rose can think about is botulism. Botox is injected into the muscles that cause wrinkles between the eyebrows and the lines that corrugate the corners of Rose's eyes. She googled it. The Botox paralyzes the muscle so that it can't contract, but after about four months it wears off and the muscle becomes active again, creases forming on Rose's face with every squeeze of the orbicularis oculi. The treatment nearly made Rose look her own age, but Lacey says Botox only works on the active wrinkles. As opposed to the inactive ones, Rose supposes, that are caused by the accelerated aging of her skin, the topography of her face changing before her eyes.

Rose schedules an appointment for Juvederm while she's on vacation. At her consultation, Lacey describes the procedure and tells her she can expect mild to medium pain for a couple days to a couple weeks afterwards. She will be careful not to hit vessels in the process. Rose will have to watch for white patches on the skin and call immediately if they occur, to have an antidote administered. This is very rare. Lacey has only seen it a couple times in her fourteen years of practice. She doesn't look more than thirty to Rose—it must work.

The day of, Rose takes four Advil for the pain a half-hour before her appointment. She turns off her cellphone in the lobby, as instructed by the welcome sign on the door, says no thanks to coffee, and sinks into the tan leather couch with a copy of *Elle Decor* while she waits. The girl on the desk brings Rose a clipboard and pen with papers for her to read and sign. When she's escorted into the treatment room, Lacey asks how her day is going and explains the risks that Rose has just consented to. Common side effects are redness, tenderness, and pain, but there are more serious things that Rose needs to be aware of. Complications can include permanent scarring, vision abnormalities, blindness, or stroke. Just this week a woman in Toronto went blind, and she's been having it done for decades by the same doctor. But like Lacey said, this is rare. Just keep an eye and call if you have any questions or concerns.

Ready?

As ready as I'll ever be.

We'll be done before you know it.

Lacey leans in and Rose catches a glimpse of the needle before it punctures her skin. She feels the stainless steel tip intruding into her skin, probing the recesses of her cheek. Lacey massages with her left index and middle fingers as she manoeuvres into the muscle around invisible veins.

You bleed easily?

No, why?

Do you take a blood thinner?

I took some Advil before I came?

Oh. That's a blood thinner. Looks like you'll have some bruising. A little more than normal. Some swelling. That's not unusual though.

Rose has a high pain threshold but low tolerance, and lower still when it's inflicted as a result of her own decision. By the time Rose plumps her pillows and piles them three high to prop herself up in bed for the night, her cheeks are mottled and puffy, the swelling in the right side of her upper lip blossoming like an ugly purple rose, the edges of its petals already wilted into a lopsided pout. She'll have to stay home while she's off, until her face goes back to normal. *The price you pay*, Rose thinks. The price you must pay. Pennies. In the scheme of things.

It's all smoke and mirrors.

God Forgive Me

I was a nutbar wasn't I, Cela. I used to be mad at people for going on with their everyday lives, hanging their wash on the clothesline, for not dying instead of Luke.

Yes, Rose, you were.

I remember driving up the road one day, going to Sobeys or somewhere. I was on the long stretch with no houses either side. I focused on a man walking on the opposite side of the road, facing traffic, my eyes boring into his back. And I remember, very distinctly thinking, *Why wasn't it you? What's the good of you? I wish it was you.* I think it was that hard ticket from out the shore, that Davis guy.

No Rose, it was Harold White.

No, girl. It couldn't be.

It was Harold, Rose.

Oh my god.

Rose had carried with her the partial memory of wishing him dead. It was foggy and insistent, tugging at her like a homeless man begging for loose change.

Oh my god. Please don't tell anyone I thought that, Cela. There's something wrong with me.

The fog dissipates, and the man Rose wished could be traded for Luke comes sharply into focus, with his bald head.

Rose had found Harold to be an unlikeable teenager. Although she never knew him very well. Harold was poor looking, a crooked front tooth combined with an overbite, and a belly like an old man, though he was not much more than a child. He talked incessantly, and his squealy voice created a whistling sound through his front teeth that grated on Rose. She found everything about him irritating, even though he was very smart in school. No doubt his mother hung on his every word, and he fully expected the world to do so as well. Rose assumed that Harold's mother knew that Harold was not pretty. That people talked about him behind his back. Harold was her only child.

When he was eighteen, Harold's speech began to slur, the spittle that always accompanied his hurried outbursts becoming drool. Harold spent months going back and forth to doctors and then the news spread around Ferndale. Benign.

> be-nign
> adjective
> : of a gentle disposition
> : showing kindness and gentleness
> : of a mild type or character that does not threaten health or life; especially: not becoming cancer
> : having no significant effect

Benign. But the rumour was they'd have to drill a hole through the side of Harold's skull, cut into the bone, and chisel it away.

When Harold came home after a month, he was bald. The hair would never grow in. Harold recovered, but if Rose was being honest, the residual effects only accentuated his negative traits, and she liked him even less than she had before.

Unspoken

Subject: Infinity
<rosetremblett@gmail.com> wrote:

So this guy last night… infinity… on and on and on about infinity… haha… get it… on and on and on haha…

So he's going on about how weird infinity is, and telling me about the "truths of infinity." And he's talking about googols and 10 to the 100, and how a googolplex is the EXACT SAME DISTANCE FROM INFINITY As THE # 1.

And did you know that HALF of infinity is INFINITY????

And also if you fully grasp infinity then you don't understand infinity and if you are not blown away by infinity then you don't understand infinity.

duh…

So of course i'm sittin there thinkin infinity is how when you're dating frogs and you come to the realization that either you are insane because you keep hoping that this frog will be different, or you have come up against the certainty that frogs are, infinitely, frogs. And i decided that either way this is gonna go on forever. That's KIND OF like infinity : ////

> **Subject:** Re:Infinity
> <cela_2000@hotmail.com> wrote:
>
> Wow… speaking of pot…
>
> Ribbit ribbit??

Subject: Re: Re: Infinity
<abbey_b@yahoo.ca> wrote:

Why the hell do you need to date frogs into infinity?!

Subject: Re: Re: Re: Infinity
<rosetremblett@gmail.com> wrote:

Abbey it's called the spice of life. Haha

Subject: Re: Re: Re:
<abbey_b@yahoo.ca> wrote:

I just don't see it.

Subject: the dance
<cela_2000@hotmail.com> wrote:

Abbey, the French have a concept called la danse. It's not about the relationship, or whether it will work or not, or how much it will work. It's the dance, the unthinking naturalness of it. Just "la danse."

Or you know… Garth Brooks… the dance… saying goodbye too soon but taking a chance and accepting the pain so as not to miss the dance. Or something like that.

Subject: Re: the dance
<abbey_b@yahoo.ca> wrote:

I totally, totally, totally agree with that! If I wanted to miss the pain of losing Jon, I'd have to miss the dance of having him for 18 years, and I couldn't let go of that to avoid any amount of pain!!

Father Jerome gave us a poem after Jon died, and it said

basically the same thing. I'll have to try to find it again.

Subject: Re: Re: the dance
<cela_2000@hotmail.com> wrote:

I know a guy in a wheelchair who grew up with polio, who says he would go through it all again, all the pain, misery, and heartbreak, to get where he is now, to be who he is.

Subject: Re: Re: Re: the dance
<rosetremblett@gmail.com> wrote:

Me too, Cela, whatever that says about me.

Subject: Re: Re: Re: the dance
<abbey_b@yahoo.ca> wrote:

Me too.

Subject: Re: Re: Re: Re: the dance
<rosetremblett@gmail.com> wrote:

Abbey, do you mean even losing Jon? You'd even lose Jon, to be who you are now?

Because I know the easy answer is "of course I would take it all back to have my son." Or my husband, or my legs, or whatever.

But I've asked myself that question.

And haven't had the nerve, in the deepest most secret part of my recesses (yes, I DO have them haha), to answer the question, even in a whisper to myself.

But I know the answer. I would not change who I am.

And I know that if it were my child instead of my husband, the answer might be different. And it's not even a question that needs answering. But still, we subject ourselves to the question, over and over. Or I do anyway.

ps: Does anyone else think that it is ironic that one of the biblical plagues was toads and that we also refer to men as frogs? I mean ironic in the Alanis Morissette sense — not ironic at all but a little bit odd or funny or something. Or maybe Ben Franklin called toads a plague, I'm not sure. Haha

Subject: Re: Re: Re: Re: the dance
<abbey_b@yahoo.ca> wrote:

Rose, you made my breath catch with that question. I can't for the life of me answer it. I never looked (outside my heart) at that question before — I always thought of the other side "that I wouldn't give up the pain of losing him, if it meant I had to give up the 18 years of having him." But when asked if I would give up who I am now, who my children are, to have him back again???!!! That's too big for me…

If I didn't believe that everything happens for a reason, and those reasons we don't know until all is said and done… If I didn't believe that everything is as it should be…

If I was willing to give up the last 18 years (yes, he's been gone 18 years!), and ask for him back again, I don't know… It would change everything about who my kids and I are today. You know? Don't think I could do that now… He's been gone 18 years and the others are here and are so precious and it's non-negotiable that I would interfere with their lives.

Amazing!!! But I guess that's my answer! I feel guilty about that, but that's what's truly in my heart. I know because I've often thought about it (inside my heart), just didn't have anyone ask me before, and never dreamed I'd have to admit it out loud. Even to myself.

Losing Jon practically killed me. I wouldn't ask to go back now though…

And I know you have deep recesses, because you couldn't ask me the questions you do, or get me to think like you do, if you didn't. I love you.

Subject: Re: Re: Re: Re: the dance
<rosetremblett@gmail.com> wrote:

There it is.

Justification.

That I'm not the only one who feels this way.

Not sure why I can't see the screen through the blur.

And aware that if I was faced with the choice at this moment, real choice, I might answer differently. But I'd be torn.

Whatever all that says…

> Subject: Re: Re: Re: Re: the dance
> <cela_2000@hotmail.com> wrote:
>
> Rose, it only says that you believe that the pain and the heartbreak are part of what makes you you.
>
> Unfortunately, it's the pain and the loss that defines so much of us. It has to, or we wouldn't be able to carry on. We cope, we make it a part of us, and we go on. It's kind of like Aunt Teish said after Luke died, "It gets better, Rose honey." But then as she went out through the door, she looked up at me and said, "But sometimes it's some fuckin' hard, b'y."
>
> But it's one of the astounding things about who we are. We typically wouldn't change it.

Subject: Re: Re: Re: Re: the dance
<rosetremblett@gmail.com> wrote:

Yes I agree. But it's forcing ourselves to admit that about tragedy that astounds me, to use your word, Cela. Everyone would say about the everyday ordinary that they wouldn't change it. But when you contemplate, even force yourself to admit, that you wouldn't change wheelchairs and lost lives, it's pretty surreal.

You know, there's the distinct possibility that we should be locked up.

> Subject: Re: Re: Re: Re: the dance
> <abbey_b@yahoo.ca> wrote:
>
> I loved Aunt Teish… still miss her when I come home… she used to be right disgusted with me being away… she said one of these days you'll come home and I'll be dead… she thought everyone should stay home : (

Crash

2015

I want to see Emily.

You what?

Rose feels a tsunami of panic wash over, waves sweeping outward from the hypocentre in her gut, spreading into her muscles and her sinew and her bones. Her breathing becomes rapid, and her heart lurches in her ribcage. Luke watches Rose's face as she opens her mouth.

You know everything then? You know about Emily? About our lives? You know I'm only visiting you here?

How'd you think it could be happening without me knowing, Rose, my love?

I don't know. I don't know. Did you know that I have to re-live that day every time I come here to visit you? Did you know that too? Did you know that and let me do it anyway?

Yes, I knew. I do too Rose. I do too.

An aftershock sweeps through Rose and she folds onto the living-room floor. He has known all along. And he wants Emily.

How could you do this? How could you not tell me? Have you tried to contact her?

She's mine too, Rose.

You came to her in her dreams. That was really you.

Rose thinks about all the times she'd wished Luke was there with her. That first winter he was gone when the power went out for four days. When Emily was in grade two and she came home from school on Father's Day with a card for Rose. When Rose walked across the stage at the university and Cela sat in the audience with Emily and Liam and Maggie. When trying to live for one more day was sometimes more than Emily could manage. Rose thinks about lying on the floor in the bathroom at the Janeway. She wished for Luke all the way up Prince Philip Drive.

She wishes she had asked him to stay home from that last trip to the Grand Banks.

You can't have her, Luke. Do you know that every visit cost me a year? Do you know that? A year that I can't spend with Emily, Luke. Emily and Liam and Maggie and our grandkids. I won't let you do this to Emily, Luke. I won't let Emily come here.

She pulls herself to her feet, steadies herself against the wall.

Rose, listen to me.

I won't come back here again, Luke.

Please don't do this, Rose. Please. I want to see her. I need to.

Rose turns her back on Luke and steps toward the door, Luke reaching for her left wrist as she goes.

Rose. Don't do this.

Rose shakes free of Luke's grasp and stumbles toward the door. She bypasses the wall where she usually leaves, and jerks the door open, the hinges giving way with a screech that is drowned out by Luke's wails.

Rose, come back here.

His voice reverberates through Rose's body as she slams the door behind her and looks back in through the oval window, then launches herself down the steps. She takes two long strides before her knees give way again, and she crawls the remaining distance to the edge of the garden, where she lies on her back, her feet flat on the ground, knees jutting to the sky. She wants to crawl under the blades of grass. She wants her father. Rose feels tremors sweep from her feet to her head.

Luke is frozen to the floor as Rose stumbles away. The slamming of the door becomes a roar of water as Rose stares in the window, Luke standing at the boat's steering wheel and watching the wave rise to its full height—as tall as a six-storey building—and crash down upon him. The top of the wheel-house is forced up and over from port to starboard, galvanized pipe stanchions sheared off like aluminum foil. The whole boat disintegrates at once, fragments scattering and pushed aside. The water's surface is littered with flotsam: pieces of the wheelhouse, port afterside, and forecastle floor; wooden slatted boxes; green and yellow dory parts; rope and twine; a section of the keel with ribs still attached. And five men. The yellow life raft explodes from its fibreglass canister on impact, inflating as it sheds the shell and bobs on the ocean's surface, like a buoy marking their location. Luke screams at the ocean as it swallows him.

EMILY!

The mermaids watch as Luke's body slowly descends in water that is colder, denser, darker. It is quieter. Luke's body drifts in slow motion with the plankton as tuna dart by. Downward through seaweed, jellyfish, and schools of dogfish, mermaids and dolphins hovering as he falls away.

Emily.

Cross

Emily sits straight-backed, chair pulled close. Her hands are prone on the table's surface, but they are not resting. Emily can still feel the wood caressing her finger last night, as she ran its tip the length of the tiny stipes and left to right across the *patibulum*. Her mother gave it to her to bring with her today, but Emily felt Rose's resistance to this venture, which she tried to cover by pulling her close, planting a kiss on the centre of her forehead.

I love you. Remember that.

She ran her flat palm down the back of Emily's hair and hugged her tight, clinging.

I need to know, Mom.

No *sedicula* to support the weight of outstretched arms. No *suppedaneum* to hold the feet. This is not a working cross. This is just a token. Carved from a stolen scrap of salvaged boat wreckage. Not more than an inch high, it has sat in a dark drawer for twenty years.

***** ***** *****

On the Tuesday after the accident, Rose and her sisters go to a Coast Guard warehouse with Luke's family and the other families to see the remains. The warehouse door pulls wide, the raucous grating of steel on steel piercing Rose's muscles and her sinew and her bones. Rose reaches for Cela's arm and squeezes her eyes shut as they are herded to the centre of the building. The cavernous echo of voices and movement and the smells of iron and bodies close together make Rose feel like she is stranded on a busy street corner far from home. When the group stops in unison Rose opens her eyes and finds herself confronted by large red tarps spread on the floor to contain the sundry remnants of Thursday.

The entire wheelhouse top with a section of the front still in one piece; it had been fitted with a guardrail, whose rails had been screw-threaded into base plates; all the rails are missing. Eight of the ten galvanized pipe stanchions are sheared off. The afterwall of the wheelhouse is intact but the door is missing. The white wall is lying flat on the red tarp. A radar scanner is intact but its dome is missing. There is a searchlight still attached to the wheelhouse; its shaft is slightly bent but its lens is not broken. White paint is scratched and missing, the dented wood scored bare in places. Rose wonders if the boat required painting on Wednesday. Two exterior lights fitted to the grey underside eave at the front of the wheelhouse are whole. Rose thinks she would like to have one to install over their new front door when she finishes the house. Smaller bits of the wheelhouse and pieces from the port afterside are strewn among the debris alongside worn wooden boxes, green and yellow dory parts, a section of the forecastle floor, ropes and twine, orange net-marking balloons, a tiny section of the keel, one brown suede sneaker.

To one side is an inflated yellow life raft with seawater sloshing in its bottom as Luke's brothers walk its perimeter, touch it, disturb it. One kneels and dips his cupped hand, then raises it and lets the holy water run through his fingers and up his arm, rivulets coursing their way past the short sleeves and through the wiry curls in his armpit, melding with the sweat there. There is a flurry of hands and voices, speculation and denial as a pair of eyeglasses passes between the brothers' hands.

Whose are they? Are they Luke's?

Are those Luke's glasses?

No. No, they're mine. The glasses are mine. I dropped them.

The brother grabs the glasses, places them on top of his head, and walks straight toward the gaping warehouse door, past the boat's broken skeleton, pocketing a shard of forecastle floor as he passes. A tiny piece of wood to give to Rose. Nothing. In the scheme of things.

*****·*****·*****

Emily parks on a side street, walks around the back of the house to a door as she was told to do. There is a sign with a smiley face that says *You're in the right spot, don't knock. Please come in and take a seat.* She opens the door and descends to a basement. Emily opens another door and she is in a small kitchen with a large round table and two chairs set on opposite sides.

Emily sits straight-backed in a chair that she pulls close to the high table. A woman enters the kitchen and remains standing behind the second chair. She looks like someone who owns a fanny pack. Not the type Emily would expect.

Hello. Before we get started let me explain a little how the session will work. It is energy based. The more open you are the more that can come across to me, and sometimes the spirit world shows me things that you may not understand immediately. Please take these things away and look for validation after you leave here.

She is swaying left to right with her eyes closed.

Tell me about a female who passed when she was still young, thirty, maybe forty.

Emily tries to correct her and explain that no females close to her have died; she visualizes the cross in her pocket in hopes of redirecting the woman. But she continues.

I think she was an aunt.

Emily takes a deep breath and looks down at the table to hide her disappointment.

She let you get away with stuff your mother never would.

Emily decides to let the woman go on.

You spent many nights at her house drinking and smoking pot together.

Emily had tried pot a couple times, but it made her so anxious and paranoid that she didn't touch it again. She smiles at the thought of lighting up with Cela or Abbey. *Yeah, no.*

Your aunt was an average-built woman, dark hair and nice long eyelashes like your own.

Emily thinks about the sixty dollars it costs her every two weeks for those lashes. The woman presses two fingers between her eyes. Explains that her headaches usually mean the passing was an accident or was unexpected. Like a car accident, or an illness. Emily wonders how else a thirty-year-old might die.

The woman feels a male presence, and Emily sits up straighter, paying attention.

A grandfather. Your father's father. Tell me about your father.

He's dead.

Oh, that's who you came here hoping to hear from. I think it's him. What was he like? Was he stern?

I don't know. I was a baby.

What did he look like? Tall? Dark hair like yours?

My hair is red, I dye it.

Well I don't know who that is then. Possibly an uncle. So your grandfather, your father's father. He was a sweet man. Caring. You were one of few, if not the only granddaughter, and you were a favourite because of that. He has left a pair of thigh-high rubber boots somewhere for you that he wants you to find. He left money after he passed that you will find. Spirit sees you getting married down south in the near future. But don't wait on him forever. If he's not ready after all this time then cut him loose. You deserve better than that.

Emily is twenty-one. She and her boyfriend just broke up. The woman walks around the table and hugs Emily's shoulders from behind.

Your father is not here.

She lays a business card beside Emily's trembling hand on the table and leaves the room.

Emily places both palms on the lip of the table and pushes herself out and up. She does not glance at the card. She cradles her belly and feels a kick as she crosses the narrow space to the door and climbs the stairs, her fingertips slipping into her pocket, grazing the edge of the miniature cross.

Acknowledgements

So many thanks to so many wonderful people I have had the blessing and good fortune to have in my corner. This novel started as a life, evolved into an idea, into a thesis, into a story. To the extraordinary community of artists and cheerleaders and sculptors of souls at Memorial University, thank you for guiding it along its way.

To Mary Dalton, where I began. I resisted her prodding to write what I know. But she was right, of course. To Rob Finley, who brought me creative non-fiction before I knew it existed and when I needed it most. Rob gave me the means to first turn my feelings into words, and he trusted me when I needed fiction to navigate the emotion. To Robert Chafe, who gave me dialogue, and a therapy shoulder with his open door and heart. To Danine Farquharson, Jennifer Lokash, and Rob Ormsby, who steered me through roiling academic waters and cheered from the sidelines. To the Naked Parade writing collective—Bridget, Jim, Heidi, Jen, and Tracy, who were there from the beginning, and the others who joined us and helped us to grow.

To Lisa Moore, who believed my words and made me believe in them myself. Lisa championed the story and put legs back under it every time I kicked them out. She refused to let it die. She refused to let me give up. Her knowledge and guidance and patience and encouragement are bottomless and are offered through gentleness and compassion.

To Bethany and Julie and the team at Goose Lane, for moulding the final product with a feather light touch, who trusted me to do what's best, who found an artist for the cover design whose work was synchronicitous with the words.

And to my daughter, Meghan Careen, who has been my eyes, my heart, and my conscience for this book. She offered reminding when I needed it that I am a vessel for the words and they will come in their time. Brave and boundless in her optimism and advice and guidance and support. Unyielding in her belief in the words and their power. And to her, Will, and Emily, who lived it with me, who allowed me to expose our wounds to the light. This is my love song to you.

And to the real Luke, Mark Traverse, whose love still sustains me nearly three decades on.